MW01698272

Kevin O Cuinn's The Coordinates Of (His) Separation *is a collection of some of the most beautifully wrought gems of story compression you will ever read, each one brilliantly capturing a moment and a feeling that takes other writers pages and pages to nail down.*
--Donald Ray Pollock, author of *Knockemstiff, The Devil All the Time & The Heavenly Table*

Disturbance spines the small stories and often quiet lives in Kevin O Cuinn's The Coordinates of (His) Separation. *Rumblings of the everyday and everyone told through stark prose and keen observation, and made odd and revelatory by O Cuinn's insistence on absurdity as commonplace (isn't it just); the active engagement of the reader; and the constancy of our yearning. In one word: Distinctive.*
--Ethel Rohan, author of *The Weight of Him, Cut Through The Bone* & *Goodnight Nobody*

A moment is a thing that you live through and then it's gone, but if you could step out of life's string of moments, exist beside time instead of in it, it'd be a little like reading these koan-like stories by Kevin O Cuinn. They work their magic in a variety of ways: short and long, lapidary, ephemeral, abstract and as deliberately concrete (as in real, as in hard) as a farmer swinging from a beam in the barn. The thing that ties all of it together is the exactitude of the prose, which is itself varied in voice, but always pitch perfect. I'm reminded of the elusive writing of Joseph Young and Russell Edson. This is a book to get deep with.
--Adam Robinson, publisher, *Publishing Genius*

Kevin O Cuinn's new collection of stories and prose reminds me of Lidia Yukvavitch's A Chronology of Water *in their most breath-sucking moments. O Cuinn's voice captures phantom desire at its most ritualistic and carnal—the enraged flirty glance from a red-haired punk girl at a green light, a silent, secret assault in church "While Oliver Paints." O Cuinn's most delicious moments exist in brutal wonder that points to the wound and asks: is that a dark bruise or rocker chick makeup?*
--Antonia Crane, author of *Spent*

Kevin O Cuinn is a sly outlier, a trickster, a pool shark of a writer, at the top of his game, running the proverbial table with 56 assorted cue ball fictions that will leave you thunderstruck. An uncategorized Irish writer, O Cuinn is—three parts Flann O'Brien, two parts Kelly Link, one part Borges, with a twist of Diane Williams. He's a talent and there are enough surprises in this collection to keep your fires burning for days.
--Richard Peabody, editor, *Gargoyle Magazine*

Kevin can write in a very special way. I love his particular type of strangeness.
--Giancarlo DiTrapano, Tyrant Books

THE COORDINATES OF (HIS) SEPARATION

-stories-

Kevin Ó Cúinn

The author wishes to thank MK & Bill, Michael Kalmes Meyers, Myra O'Mahony, Hugo Pratt, Corto Maltese, Joseph Campbell, Kathryn Rantala, Cooper Renner, Jackie Corley, Karl Hubener, Don G, Sergio Kun Agüero, Grace Paley, Jack Yeats, Connemara, Jarod Roselló, Grace O'Malley, Word Riot, Saint-Lunaire, Steve Finbow, Lee Klein…George, Nuha, & Charlotte Cabrera LaChance.

Support Small Presses & Independent Booksellers

Original cover artwork and design by Jarod Roselló

ISBN: 978-0-9985463-7-7
LCCN: 2017949731

FIRST EDITION

Published by
Ravenna Press
(ravennapress.com)

Contents

for Andrea

Prelude

It read 'I have sent you a song.' That was it: six words on a blank postcard. No name, no stamp. An advertiser's ruse, I supposed, but for what I did not know. Otherwise, coupons from Aldi, a flyer from an Italian place. I turned to the stairs, thought I heard a glockenspiel. I put it down to tiredness; I was tired and looking forward to spending the evening on the couch with Wolf—Wolf Blass—which is a Merlot and not some guy. Actually, it's a wine made by a guy of the same name so technically, yes, Wolf Blass is a guy.

My building was a dump. The linoleum in the stairwell curled where it should have kissed the wall. The walls flaked. As I walked up to the eighth floor, sounds I didn't associate with the building grew: the picking and strumming of strings, also drums, and either a soprano sax or a clarinet, I never can tell. A sad guitar. On the sixth floor, a cataractous eye in the crack of a door, but nothing new in that.

Eighth floor, quiet, fourth door left. Home. I pressed my ear to the door. Though the music had stopped there were people in there, definitely, hushing and shuffling. There were no signs of a forced entry so Maud must have given them the spare, I supposed. I was not being burglarised. Someone leaned back in my creaky chair; throats were cleared. Then what sounded like a baton being tapped in conductorly fashion. Silence. I turned the key and pushed the door.

Crossing

She points, cocks her thumb; he slows. He's irate—shouts, brakes; she stops. She recognises the plates, then him. She retracts the faux pistol, flashes the finger, walks. He'll realise later, then google her, call someone they used to know. The someone they used to know will do the same. Memories ripple away from the crossing. She steps into a shop; a bell rings.

Saturday in Hackney

I was wondering how you were getting on. If you were getting on. So I tapped some keys and there you were, in your long CV and short hair.

I was wondering what had become of you. If you'd posted somewhere that I was forgiven. That it was okay to pick up the phone. Then I saw your message, the one that said I should stop by.

I was wondering how differently we saw the past. And the present, the subjunctive. So I took the bus to Hackney, past the shell that was the petrol station, the Kurdish barber, halal butcher, to the pub at the end. Of course, at the end. I wondered what would happen first, would the door open or would the bus come back into view.

The Magic Word

And then somebody said the magic word. Whale. It echoed and bobbed up and down the beach, and into the dunes, where I was relieving Victoria of her secrets.

'Whale,' she hummed, 'whale..'

'False alarm—for sure—again, ' I told her, nuzzling previously uncharted waters.

'No. Go, please, check. '

So I did. And there they were, a quarter mile out, a pod of pilot whales.

We'd spent three weeks at the ocean, waiting for a sighting. Which wasn't long, compared to the fourteen weeks I'd waited, before she let me put my hand up her skirt.

The whales moved so graciously, like an old freight train. The younger ones to the rear, grandstanding for the cameras. I'd never witnessed anything so beautiful, and doubted I ever would again.

'And?' said Victoria, clipping her bra, 'and?'

'Just like I said, false alarm. You can relax.'

'Again,' she sighed.

'Yeah,' I said, and returned to the sandy crevices.

Lunch

She finds Dim Sun translated into five European languages. *Toccando il Cuore. Das Herz berühren. Tocar el corazón. Toucher le Coeur.* Touch the heart. It was his idea to eat here. She rotates the menu to admire the pictograms: she sees hats and umbrellas and a girl, much younger than she is, cycling down a country lane.

The Orange Grove

There was no gate to the orange grove, just ancient mossy walls, held together by time.

'Hold this,' she said, untying her sari and handing it to me. 'Mimi says the heathens consecrated the grove to their gods, before the Buddha. Long before'

Yellow like the sun, I draped the sari around my neck, battling not to look at what it had unveiled. She reached above and took hold of the wall. She placed her toes in a groove, stepped up and reached again.

My hands shadowed her pantied behind.

'What-are-you-doing?' she said, staccato, her head tucked under her arm.

'In case you fall,' said I.

'You wish,' said she, and smiled, 'oh, but how you wish.'

It's true, I did wish. I'd never wished for anything more.

She moved with the grace of a ballerina, and reached the top in eight moves.

'What are you waiting for?' she called down, 'soon it will be dark.'

I grunted my way up, my belly heavy with tender seasoned lamb—cardamom and mustard seed and wild, thick-stemmed fennel. From atop the wall I heard soft muffled laughter. 'You have the wrong muscles for climbing,' she said. 'Your muscles are from the fitness studio—nice to look at, but no good for climbing.'

She dusted dirt from her hands then lowered herself into the orange grove. I shook out the sari and released it into the sky. It hovered for a heartbeat, then twisted and crumpled and fell—into her reach in orange tree shade. It was then, as the sky clapped with thunder, that the ancient wall rumbled below me, and as the ground approached, I clutched the void above.

Laundry

She slips the shirt over a hanger, notices the label for the first time: FABRIQUE AU MACAO. They'd bought it in a shop off the market. He'd tried to impress with his school French, had assumed that they'd have school French, too. The owner handed him a calculator, they passed it back and forth. The owner's daughter served tea. He said, *C'est beaucoup,* four times before they agreed; she'd counted. She shakes her head at the memory, then closes the top button and walks to the wardrobe.

Nancy Spain

There's a big old espresso machine behind the bar and nobody speaks when it's in action because it sounds like a steam train in full throttle. France, 1987. It's where, when, I meet Le Grecque.

Le Grecque had left his island, Samos, and come to France on his way to fight Franco in Spain. He said it like that, 'To fight Franco, ' like it was personal, just the two of them. Nineteen thirty something. It's where, when, Le Grecque meets an Irish girl, Nancy. His eyes say S t u f f. The machine hisses, pumps.

'I stayed,' he says 'and Nancy continued on, to Spain,' We fan our hands through steam like we're waving her goodbye.

Nancy fights Franco. She lives through it all, marries, is widowed and inherits a small hotel. She writes a book called A Hotel in Spain.

'All before you were born. Perhaps before your father was born. In the book there was a man: The Greek,' he says. 'He took a bullet in Seville and died in Nancy's arms. So long ago. I used to love how her eyes conspired with the lines at her mouth; how her voice was so piano.'

Algorithm for Meshing Scenarios

You were busy on your PhD—field guide in common parlance—your how to Determine Triangle Sizing Adaptive to Curvature of Input Surfaces. There was a moment (fragile, fleeting) in which I was *this* close to understanding wtf you were talking about. You were busy on your quest to maintain smooth gradation, you said, busy on a crusade to prevent poor quality triangles from being created. Quests and crusades and adventures all sounded like fun times and I was happy to tag along a while. But after said while, said quests etcetera only equated to fun times in whatever universe you had absconded to, least not in mine. It was like you were speaking Tolkien, some lesser known dialect of Elf. Clear was, we were headed nowhere rapid, so I started planning my withdrawal, to a soon-to-be future sans geometry. I grew sideburns and considered my wardrobe. Then you told me you'd made the breakthrough—that the next step would be prototype implementation that could generate meshes from other meshes, that would *preserve and annotate sharp features ahead of time!* I tasted your excitement; your eyes blazed and the sex was otherworldly. And I couldn't help myself and didn't try, much as I'd rehearsed the monologue about us being a renegade vector—lost/without magnitude—and told you I'd be there, that I was looking forward to the ride.

Putting Down Roots in Boppard on The Rhine

We'd been saving up for a down payment, a little something with a garden. I thought. And therein lay the crux: I was ready to nest-build; Sue still had itchy feet.

'I mean, what are we anyway, birds?' she said. 'Nest. I ask you.'

We'd met in a Genealogy class, where we discovered that having Irish great-grandparents entitled us to Irish passports, hence freedom to live and work anywhere in the European Union. We were out of there as quick as you could say Deoxyribonucleic acid.

We plotted our trip from west to east, from one graveyard to the next, from the western most tip of Ireland to the north of Poland via Wales, England, Belgium, Spain, Luxembourg and Germany. There were births and deaths in dusty ledgers—and sometimes headstones to match the names—but mostly our ancestors' plots had long since been turned over. We recorded what details we found and moved on, by bus, by train, sometimes we hitched. The search for our past was a search for the future, for a place of our own. We earned what money we could along the way: we picked grapes in Spain and apples in Normandy, taught English (to Belgians in Antwerp) for three weeks (when we were discovered—neither of us had a clue), we did eleven shifts at a kraut pickling factory in Poland.

It was on the trail of a Huguenot, the last space on Sue's family tree, that we discovered Boppard on The Rhine. We'd been on the road for months and were tired of moving, and of hostels; of sleeping with our valuables in our sleeping bags.

'Boppard on The Rhine. As good a place as any to put down roots,' I said.

'As in, like, dig a hole?' said Sue.

'But wouldn't it be fitting—to settle in the birthplace of Johannes Bierbaum, the one who took the boat to the promised land?'

'Nah,' said Sue, 'nah, really not.'

We found work at a place called Lorelei's Rest. Sue chambermaided, I KP'ed. We bunked in a shed out back. Klaus, the owner, called the shed 'Le Chalet', he was a real comedian. We shared the shed with Kit and Kat, an Australian couple who ran the bar, and an Hungarian guy, Laszlo. Laszlo was Head Chef, or Only Chef, and spent most of the time sobbing on his bed. No one knew why, as everyone was monolingual, the Australians exceptionally so.

After six months of working and saving, Sue was coming round to my idea of settling down. I thought.

'Come down to the pier,' she said down the phone. 'I want to show you a little something we just bought.'

We'd agreed to consult each other on anything costing more that €10, so I wasn't overly worried that she'd bankrupted us.

'This is what you call a little something?' I said, looking at the barge.

'Three grand,' she said. 'Where would you get it?'

'eBay?'

'Not even close,' she said. 'A mine.' She said mine like it was a magic word. 'And that's what we're going to call it,' she continued. 'Mine. Don't you just love homophones?'

'Sue, correct me, ' I said, 'but weren't we looking for something with a foundation? Something, like, more stationary? And, eh … weren't we going to consult, before making mayor purchases?'

'Yes, yes, and yes,' she said. 'But come on, you never would have agreed.'

I answered her with a speechless kind of look; she rolled up her sleeves like she was getting ready to fight.

'But,' I said, finally, 'but, but—'

'The engine needs work,' she said, and disappeared below.

Her head reappeared.

'Don't just stand there at the sulkathon. Do stuff.'

'But—' I said, my arms still firmly folded.

'You know how a broom works, yes? Well, I suggest you take it out of your ass and put it to its proper use.'

So maybe it wasn't the right time to settle down. Or maybe Boppard on The Rhine wasn't the right place? But, but the girl was the right girl, that was something I was in no doubt of. Not really in any doubt of.

Okay, I wondered a little.

A stubborn layer of tar sat on the surface of the deck. The result, I supposed, of decades of dirty boots. Between shifts at Lorelei's, I brushed and hosed the deck, then I scraped and brushed it again, and hosed, twice, three times. But apart from the calories I burned, the whole endeavour was a waste of time; the tar took on the consistency of gunge, it stuck to everything. Sue sighed a lot, when she surfaced from the engine room, but was otherwise reticent. Below deck, it took me fifteen hours to strip the living quarters of red wallpaper and blue linoleum. The previous owners were French. I used the linoleum to cover the deck-gunge.

'Good move,' said Sue, from around a door. The engine still sounded a lot like emphysema.

Klaus, Laszlo, Kit and Kat passed by regularly, like they were involved in some kind of relay between the dock and Lorelei's Rest. They'd wave, and raise thumbs in encouragement. It was good to see Laszlo getting out, he even baked a pie once, a fish thing with mashed potatoes on top, and cheddar on top of that; smoked herring had never tasted so good. Kit and Kat helped out too, Kat sewed curtains for the portholes, Kit gave me lessons in using Klaus' power tools. In Australia, he explained, it's on the curriculum at the kindergarten.

I turned my attention to the sleeping quarters, somehow doubting that our houseboat would ever be a love-boat. The walls were adorned with pages from bygone magazines. They showed coal mines and miners, refineries, slack heaps, and yellowed pin ups of Samantha Fox.

Then it happened. First there was silence, complete silence, the first in a month. I guessed the engine had died, but then it began to hum, softly, and the humming grew, and grew some more, until it purred like a loved-up tomcat. And there she was in the door, Sue. She looked good, greased-up in overalls, wrench in one hand, cigarette in the other.

'I'm impressed,' I said, 'you really showed that sucker.'

Inhaling deep on the cigarette, she kicked off her Caterpillars and let her overalls fall to the floor. There was nothing much underneath in way of clothing.

'I want to test a theory,' she said, 'that winners have better sex.'

'And?' I said after.

'It was good,' said Sue, smoking again. 'But fixing the engine was better.'

'I didn't realise you were mechanically inclined,' I told her. 'You're just, just … so full of surprises.'

'Oh, yeah,' she said, looking all mysterious.

We planned our exit from Boppard for the end of Carnival, German Mardi Gras; Fasching in the vernacular. We'd follow the Rhine till it met the Danube and go east till Europe ended. Until then, there would be little rest at the Lorelei. Clubs and fraternities had booked the place out, some of them years in advance. I learned that Germans take Carnival and being silly very seriously. For two long weeks, 24/7, Boppard on The Rhine was firmly in the hands of revellers of a different rub, most dressed as clowns. Which was unfortunate—monks, but especially clowns, never fail to freak me out. And here I was in Rednose, formerly known as Boppard. Of course clowns have to eat and drink and shop and park the car somewhere, just like normal folk. But seeing them do everyday stuff was especially disturbing. I was continually startled: one standing in line at the checkout, another eating bratwurst, or smoking outside a bar, or sitting mournfully over a beer; that one sicko pushing an empty pram and singing a lullaby. Actually, the mournful one in the bar was kind of okay. Others: driving, jogging by the water, holding hands, kissing. Kissing with tongue in clown regalia. I hadn't learned a lot of German, but did have a soft spot for words that couldn't be translated directly into English—*fernweh* was one of them: the opposite of homesick. I was ready to leave Boppard on The Rhine.

I spent what time I could working on Mine. It—Sue insisted on *She*—was almost inhabitable, but we put off moving in until we would cast off for good. I was now adept in the use of the electric sander. Klaus got us a deal on varnish, the place began to smell of class.

The time came for us to say our goodbyes to Lorelei's Rest. There was schnapps and there were hugs, Laszlo baked that pie again. The whole evening was a complete anti-climax, we were in bed by eleven.

'Passport, cash, condoms?' checked Sue.

'Affirmative.'

'I guess we're ready then,' she said.

'I guess we are. Goodnight my love.'

'Goodnight,' she said. 'It's been a blast.'

I woke at ten, unsure of my whereabouts—or even my origins—and rolled onto the floor, clutching my head.

I should have seen it coming, the thought that rose and sobered me—she's gone. Second and third thoughts did not delay: she's taken Mine; I've been duped. My next thought was that a word like *duped* did not sound at all like me. I was quite sure I'd never used it before. Then it hit me: the realisation that I cared more for my investment than I did for her.

I felt guilty ten minutes later, at the pier, the barge still there. Sue'd spike a guy's drink, but she wasn't a thief. There was a Post-it stuck in a porthole: I'm gone, I'm sorry. I'm taking Laszlo with me. Bet you never guessed. This isn't about you. It's about me. Auf wiedersehen.

Full of surprises, always with the surprises.

I showed the note to Klaus, Kit and Kat.

'There's no way you could have seen it coming, mate,' said Kit, his arm around my shoulder. 'Nobody could have, it sucks.'

'This means I'm short of staff,' said Klaus. 'If you're interested in staying on, I could train you up to Head Chef. Think about it. Boppard on The Rhine is as good a place as any to put down roots.'

Little Red-Haired Girl Sighting

The Little Red-Haired Girl was all grown up. She'd just stepped outside the bar when I saw her. It sure had been a long time. She looked like a little, red-haired Joan Jet. The rock-chick-look rocked. There was a hint of something else in her hair, a touch of something added, not quite auburn, not quite I don't know what, but fancy-salon prices, for sure, sure as hell. She didn't see me on the bus across the street. I waved, and mouthed, 'It's me, Chuck,' but I guess her view was obstructed. She was busy with her props, phone in one hand, cigarette in the other. She leaned toward some stranger, holding up the cigarette. He cusped his hands around a flame and she bent slowly into it; she didn't even say thank you. I thought I saw a golden-blue bruise on her cheek but maybe it was rock-chick make-up. The last of the passengers boarded the bus, just as the light turned red again. I didn't mind though, and watched her, The Little Red-Haired Girl, smoking and talking on the phone, looking nowhere. She was even prettier now than then, prettier now than when. We got a green as she was finishing her call. She blew the last of the smoke skyward, dropped the butt ceremoniously to the ground and lifted a big black boot. And then she crushed the life out of it. Looking up for a moment, I thought she would see me, but I guess she didn't. The bus pulled away and I craned my neck back. I saw 'Ali' written in diamond studs across the back of her leather and wondered if it was supposed to mean that she was The Greatest. A gorilla held the door open and made some comment as she passed back into the bar, but she didn't respond. She didn't even look at him.

The Makings of Our Story

People remember the day we met as the day frogs and other small amphibians, also squirrels, rats, and at least one mutt—a mongrel pup called Spitz—fell from the sky. When I saw the racoon hit you in the head I pulled over and rolled down the window. I don't normally stop for hitch-hikers, you can never be sure.

'You okay?' I called, and held up a questioning thumb. In hindsight, okay, this was dumb. You were clutching a tree in a storm and a racoon had just hit you in the head. The forecast had promised rain, increasing in the afternoon, maybe a little snow on high ground, but nothing like this. The twister had sucked up the smaller life-forms of the region, spat them out all over, and moved on. And how. It moved across the horizon like a coked-up Cohiba. But here, the worst was over. A toad splayed across the windscreen, dead. The worst was mostly over. The racoon slipped into a corn field.

'Do I look the fuck okay?' you said—I thought you said—it could have been anything, the acoustics were lousy out there. I opened the passenger door and you arrived on the next gust, the tips of your toes barely touching the ground. Angry wind slammed the door behind you.

'Made it,' I said, and offered a high-five, which you didn't notice.

'I've just been hit in the head by a racoon,' you said, between gulped breaths.

'Yeah,' I said, and if I laughed I really didn't mean to, and apologise, again.

'You think that's funny?' you said.

'No, hell no,' I said. But it was funny, actually. It was funny then and I can't imagine it becoming unfunny anytime soon.

'I'm sure we'll look back and laugh about this in—'

'Don't!' you said. 'Don't presume to think we will stay in contact after this orfuckingdeal. Because we won't. I appreciate the ride, really I do, but all I'm interested in is getting to the next town.'

Though visibly, the racoon had left you unscathed, I wondered if you might be in shock. You looked ahead, poker-faced, and we sat there as the weather stormed. I told you my name and tried to take your mind of things with some small talk.

'Weather, huh?' I said.

'We should get out of here,' you said.

'We should,' I said, and moved into first.

'Now would be a good time to fasten your seatbelt,' I said. You rolled your eyes and poked at the radio. Static. I was about to offer you my Tom Waits cassette when the clock lodged in the windscreen. 11:55. Neither of us said anything but I couldn't help thinking that 11:55 was an ominous kind of time. I checked my watch, I was officially late.

Driving, driving my '76 Capri at least, was like doing the doggy paddle in a vat of refried beans. With the wind behind us and my foot on the brake, we were pushed along at a steady 15mph. You didn't say a word the whole time; just sat there, low in the seat with folded arms and a pout. A refrigerator zipped by and spilled its contents in our path.

'Hungry?' I said. Nothing.

'Who keeps bananas in the fridge?' I said. More nothing. Maybe you weren't used to other people, or were unfamiliar with the finer points of hitch-hiking, like telling the driver your name and saying, 'Thanks for stopping.' Maybe you— 'Would you take your feet off the dash, if you don't mind?' I said. Yeah, maybe not too used to other humans.

We arrived in The Hamlet of Greendale.

The Hamlet of Greendale was only a hamlet in name, it had grown some. But, still, it had a Walnutty Grove feel—had had—last time I'd been there, but not anymore. I'd had a celebratory omelette in a diner after the trial had been adjourned. It looked like an omelette but in reality it was an aberration, an insult to omelettes everywhere, despite the cheese, the bacon, the onions, the 'shrooms. But there's a time and a place so I didn't mention any of this, and looked at you, to check if you were still breathing; you yawned.

Every structure in THOG—which was how the waitress who served the omelette had referred to The Hamlet of Greendale—'First time in THOG?'—every house, church, shop and school had been levelled. In the street, the mangled remains of the burger joint's arches brought the first stage of our journey to an end.

'Time to abandon vehicle,' I said. 'There, under the courthouse, the bunker.'

'Courthouse? What courthouse?'

'Well, there used to be a courthouse above that sign down the steps to 'The Bunker?' Think you can make it?'

You stepped into the street and moved to the front of the truck, where the gust got you. I'd exited downwind, luckily, and caught you in my arms. You'd still be travelling, probably, if I hadn't. The wind knocked us ass over tit, across the street and into the entrance of the bunker. Eight ball, corner pocket. That's how it felt, like the elements were playing pool with us. Your hair smelt of bergamot.

The citizens of THOG were less than impressed at our arrival. Three of them battled to shut the heavy iron door behind us. One of them wore a 'Gatekeepers,' tee-shirt, a local trash metal band. Inside, around the entrance, people looked up, then away. I learned later that they'd lost Leroy Fulda in the last attempt to close the door. He'd be found later, dead and bloated, four miles offshore.

'Move along now, folks,' someone said. 'No loitering.'

It was difficult to tell how far back the bunker's passageway went. It was thick with people. They shuffled forward, holding candles and torches, gas lights. They were neighbours, family, colleagues, friends, and now, as one, victims.

'Plenty of room out back,' someone called from behind.

A small round man with a shining pate and wire-rimmed glasses held out a meaty hand. I guessed he was the mayor.

'Howdy-doody, citizens' he said. The weather wasn't going to spoil his good cheer. 'Welcome to THOG. This here bunker is the former wine cellar of Reinmund Becker, a German winemaker and one of our town's founders. He arrived here in 1878 with stalks and stems and the shirt on his back. The stalks and stems loved the dry acidic earth, a love affair that continues to the present day. For the first half of the twentieth century our wine cellar was also the town jail. The walls are three feet thick. But because there's no natural light, use as a jail was discontinued in 1962. Of late, The Bunker's been a bar.'

It sounded like an interesting story but his timing was all wrong. You were still beside me, but moving. I thanked the mayor and excused us. He turned to the door and welcomed more newcomers—an elderly couple and a shivering pup, the cutest thing I'd ever seen. You were ahead of me now. Afraid I would lose you, I reached out for your hand. You took it without thinking—or not—then shook it away. I curled my arm around your shoulder, but you lifted it over your head and were gone, into the labyrinth of caves and tunnels and God knows. I watched as you weaved your way through the throng, then let go a 'Hey,' wishing I'd pushed you on your name, and followed.

For you, the crowd parted smoothly, conducted you further, then closed seamlessly, as if it were a life-form. No sooner had I breached the crowd, was I ejected. Breach, eject, breach. Expelled, expunged like a foreign body: unwelcome. 'Could I just... if you don't mind, excuse me, excuse me, excuse me...' The wall of citizens of THOG was insurmountable, un-penetrate-able. I dallied at the edges, then noticed my lawyer in deep conversation with the judge. I backed away but I'd already caught their attention.

'There won't be no trial today, son,' he called to me. 'I'll ring as soon as the phone lines are fixed.'

'Trial?' said a smug citizen, and pushed his infant child behind his legs.

'A stalking thing,' I said. 'Nothing serious, a misunderstanding.'

'You want a seat?' said a woman from behind me. She picked up the pup from the bench and placed it on her lap. I hesitated for a second, the seat she'd made free was between herself and the old dude she'd come in with. The heck, you were gone; I thanked her and sat. The old man held a cigarette to his lips.

'Don't even think about it,' said the woman. 'We don't want to inhale your poison.'

He lit up anyway, blew smoke to the ceiling and eyed her with contempt. 'That's a twister out there, Eleanor Daley, and you're worried about second hand smoke?'

'Excuse my husband,' said Eleanor. 'He was born without decorum.'

Eleanor and Nathaniel were lifelong citizens of THOG. Nat was a local artist who'd exhibited in places as far away as places I still knew. Eleanor was a psychiatric nurse and breadwinner. They'd fished the puppy out of a barrel of rainwater in their yard.

'We thought about calling him Spitz,' said Eleanor, stroking the dog in her lap.

'After the swimmer,' said Nat.

'That's a lot of name for a little fella,' I said. Spitz looked at me and stretched.

'You should introduce him to your girlfriend,' said Eleanor. 'Where'd she go?'

'Chicks cream themselves within five paces of a puppy dog,' said Nat.

'Nathaniel Arnold,' said his wife. 'I will not tolerate that kind of language.'

Nat spat. Eleanor looked at the gob of sputum on the dark ground; Spitz, too, seemed interested.

'She's not my girlfriend,' I said. 'She's a hitch-hiker.'

'Is she now?' said Eleanor. 'Isn't that something?'

'Huh?' said Nat.

'What?' said I.

'I mean it's romantic, is all,' said Eleanor. 'Come on now, I can see the shine in your eyes.'

'You got the hots for her, boy?' said Nat. 'Which one is she?'

'She went off to scout the joint,' I said. 'She'll be back in a while.'

Eleanor and Nat looked at me.

'Show her the dog, son,' said Nat. 'Can't hurt to try.'

'No. I don't think so.'

'Why not?'

'It would be a pretty kitsch thing to do.'

'So you're not that interested, huh?'

'I guess not,' I said, and smiled, and shook my head in a kind of affirmation. Old Nat had nailed it. I just wasn't that interested. We had the makings of a good story, perhaps, at least a beginning. And we had arrival, then of course separation, all elements of good yarns. And I had Nat and Eleanor, benevolent strangers with their gift of Spitz. But that was all. I wasn't that interested. And anyway, I'd learned my lesson.

'Here,' said Nat, and held out Spitz.

Spitz yapped—he hadn't got his bark down yet—and wagged his tail like a pro.

'What the fuck,' I said, and tucked him under my arm, 'it can't hurt to try.'

When We Needed To Get Out More

We ate trout for dinner, fresh from the lake. 15 of them, 7 of us; they didn't stand a chance. We filled them with spinach and smothered them with butter. Then we baked them till their skins cracked and theirs eyes burst. You said they were scrum-diddlyumptious, and everyone laughed. But I was watching: you only picked. Somebody had prepared a salad; the dressing wasn't nearly as good as yours. The boys drank beer, the girls drank wine. We watched a TV movie and I laughed the whole way through, because it wasn't funny, although it tried so very hard to be. You spent a lot of time gazing high and left, up where the wall met the ceiling. Nothing much but your eyes moved for the duration. I went back for more fish, and when I dropped some on the floor, the dog wolfed it down. *He'll be sick,* you said.

We left after midnight, hugging hosts and promising it wouldn't be long until the next time. You were busy with your nails on the drive home, until—

'We need to get out more,' you said.

'Huh?' I said, 'got a problem with my friends? Don't like them?'

'No,' you said, as the wipers pushed the rain away, 'not at all.'

'Great. But they're my oldest friends,' I said.

'That's no defence,' and then you did that thing with your eyes. 'You're quite the square circle. Seriously, we need to get out more.'

Cheese Fondue

'If Hitchcock had used robins or sparrows or budgies,' he says, 'The movie would have been a damn sight more ominous.'

Watch out, Hitchcock, she says, inside.

'Or parrots, screeching Who's your Mommy?'

She nods, thinks about food.

'You going to shower?' he says, smiles.

The wind pounds the cabin.

The clock on the wall is set for another time zone. Or the battery is dying. She remembers another hike, the one with her ex-ex; she remembers the cheese fondue, how they'd dunked burger and sliced white bread and shared a pint bottle of Heineken; she remembers not wanting to leave.

'We should sleep,' she says. 'It's getting late.'

Sweet September

We sha-la-la'd all summer long, just us—you and me—and him and her and them, and their entourage of bleeding heart vegan liberals. When it got too crowded we exited in accordance with The Formula, a series of variables, most of which concerned time: time available vs. time spent, opening & closing times, time in relation to the position of certain—you never said which—stars in the southern hemisphere's night sky (relative to the compound interest on your savings account), plus other stuff I didn't get or could only describe as ephemera. The variables didn't make a lot of sense to me. But I wasn't doing the math, all said—The Formula was something you'd worked on since forever, and you had the patent to prove it. I trawled the internet and couldn't find trace of anything remotely remote—if it was empirically based it was top-secret empirically-based, And that's exactly the type of world we live in, you said. But you assured me, even promised, that it was real and out there, its bones, its marrow, its DNfuckingA. And I believed you, or I believed as much as I understood, I tried hard; who wouldn't, the sha-la-la was good and getting better.

Formulas in general: math, science, you name it, were one of our themes, a constant, a thing we discussed, but from different angles—you loved them and I didn't, and I told you so whenever I could. It's dumb, I said, who needs to know this apart from teachers? Teachers whose only function is to terrorise children. You sighed, said, In your opinion formulas are dumb but keep it to yourself—if you say it loud, people will think that you're … never mind. Then you added, But hey, it's a free world and life is short. Free? I said, *ha*. Short, yes, okay—but free? Never. In your opinion, you said. You said that often, like every time I exhausted one breath and started in on another. But we were exchanging opinions is all, we told each other, or maybe I just told you. It wasn't like we were arguing—we never really argued—we just disagreed on stuff as people do when they are close and, on occasion, intimate; it wasn't like we'd compromise the sha-la-la, much, though too much time was spent discussing its parameters, I thought, and said so. In your opinion, you answered.

The other thing outside The Formula that caused friction, was my standing up when you entered a room. Least after the first couple dozen times. Will you so fucking stop doing that, you'd say. I was against stopping, but did after your One more time and it's schluss with the you-know-what. It wasn't like I was dumb, I knew what you-know-what was code for—you just didn't say it because the entourage was about. But I could never stop the itch to stand, it was how I'd been raised. And I remember how you liked it that first time, and I still remember your laugh, it was fairy dust, insofar as I imagined fairy dust sounding. Do you mean sawdust? you said, as in the by-product of metal teeth ripping through wood at high velocity? No, I said, That's not what I mean, I mean fairy dust insofar as I can imagine fairy dust sounding—not having met any real actual fairies. That's what your laugh is to me. Real actual fairies? you said. That's so fucked up. In your opinion, I said. Oh yeah, you said. In my opinion.

The sha-la-la always had a certain edge to it after we'd had one of our divergences in opinion. *Of* opinion, you said. It was a more-good-than-bad-edge, I thought, though you disagreed, so we agreed to disagree.

The Formula, though, worked less and less as Summer became older and more crowded—him and her and their etcetera*s*—even you were having trouble working it out, even after you revised the variables and reregistered the patent, having added the thing about what song was playing at 11.59PM on any given Thursday on Radio Nova, and if the bassist was wearing a wool hat. Nova, I laughed, isn't that foreign for no-go? Face it, I said, The Formula has crashed and died. That's a heap, you said, The Formula's fine, and what do you anyway know about anything? Hmm. It was a question that gave proverbial pause for proverbial thought … Well, I began, I know—but you interrupted, It was rhetorical, you said. You know, rhetorical? Now there was a thing I actually did know stuff about, to be honest, and I would have told you, had you still been in the vicinity, and had I been able to find you—and I looked, really I did, for what was left of Summer, until the sky was constant pastel, and sweet September was undeniable.

minimal pair(s)

She tells him
to sail
his shit along.

Ship, he says,
and casts off.

While Oliver Paints

I've been sleeping with the vicar since November four years ago. The reason I went there in the first place, the church, was to get out of the rain. Years had passed since ever I'd set foot in one, though I used to go often as a girl. Later I'd go annually, just, to confess mishaps and misdemeanours, though there was never anything on my conscience that would jeopardise any kind of heaven, I think.

I was sure it was a Catholic—the bell, the stained glass—and I was looking left and right for the confession box when up comes the vicar, me thinking him a priest, and not a bad-looking one. So I asked, and he smiles and nods and tells me that my indiscretions are between myself and The Almighty, and quotes something from the Book of Timothy. 'Thanks anyway,' I said, 'and sorry,' though I don't know for what. I was on the point of turning, could feel my weight shifting right to left, when he said, 'Join me in the sacristy for a cup of tea and a fig-roll. I'll be happy to listen to anything you have on your mind.' Fig-roll indeed. One moment he was holding my hand, then stroking it, patting it, telling me to go on, to not stop, next I was flung across the table and he was inside me, thrashing like he was trying to take out a wall. The kettle hadn't even boiled.

He used to sob after, the vicar, used to ask me what Oliver would think or say or do, and go on and on. 'Don't worry your head,' I'd say, and try to console the poor sod. It's funny how roles reverse. Oliver, for the record, wouldn't bat an eyelid; what we have doesn't enter that kind of territory. Oliver paints, is all.

These days, I arrive and the tea's already poured and I'll unbutton my coat and anything that lies below—unclip, loosen, remove—and, well, it's the way things are, the way things have become between me and the vicar. The quiet after is soft but if it goes on too long the scratching starts in my head, Oliver scratching the canvas with his pinsel, and there are moments it becomes so loud that I think it will rip the world in two, that a wave will take us all, and I'll tell the vicar to fold his arms around me, to hold me awhile, till the afternoon turns dark.

One-way to Rio

The band's previous singer got some Old Time Religion and just couldn't—anymore—sing stuff that condoned and sometimes encouraged shoplifting, weed and giving head. Judith assured them she had no issue. There had been other applicants, the guys told her: Marina and Maud. Maud had ties and couldn't tour, Marina could tour but couldn't sing. Judith said she could do both, and if they were nice she'd do them too. The whole age thing though, one of them said, We kinda wanted someone our age. She asked if they knew Virginia Plain and started in before they could answer; *Baby Jane's in Acapulco, we are flying down to Riooooo.* They were sold, all four—two lead guitars, bass and drums. Is your passport valid? Both of them, she said. They laughed, said Good one, you're in. High-fives and Heinekens. How'd you hear about us? She'd seen the ad in the supermarket, on the wall beside the wanted posters. Her year book picture; so much younger then.

The Night of The Fire

Seeing him the first time. She sees him the first time—the white underweared back of him—crawling along the smoke-filled corridor. Sonja sees Marcus. She hopes he's going the right way and crawls behind, to the emergency exit, to the fire-escape. The fire-escape with the busted ladder. Alarms pierce the night and Sonja greets Marcus, she holds out a hand. Marcus takes her hand and shakes, up-down, twice, three times. They say their names but nothing else, then turn and grip the railing. They stretch their necks into the night, and below to the street. People have gathered in varying states of undress. Fire-truck sirens approach from the east. Sonja wonders if anyone remains inside, waiting for a hero, and looks at Marcus; Marcus smiles. Smoke billows. Flames lick curtains in broken windows, curtains flutter and fall. They wait. Rain starts to fall. It is soft and playful and teases the fire; the rain stops. A ladder climbs to a halt in the air beside them. How you folks doing? says the fireman. He extends an arm and Sonja grips. She clambers over the railing. Marcus follows. For a heartbeat only air below. The fireman has mustard on his chin. Colleagues on other ladders hose water. Sonja waves to them as they descend.

Standing in the car park. Sonja sips tea from a plastic cup, Marcus stands beside her. Sonja wishes she weren't wearing her Miss Kitty pyjamas. Sonja has large glassy eyes and the complexion of a porcelain doll, smudged albeit, with dirt. Her hair is speckled with ash. Marcus places a blanket around her shoulders and tells her there is no point in catching a cold. Marcus shivers; Sonja extends her arm and the blanket around his shoulder. They huddle till the shivering stops, then huddle anyway, For morale, says Marcus. A fleet of ambulances speeds people away, a hearse arrives. Marcus sees a blackened hand fall from a stretcher, Don't look, he tells Sonja, though he knows she will.

The line to get a new room. The line to get a new room is at the hotel across the street. Ironically, the new hotel has just reopened after a fire. The fire alarm hums to a halt; a communal sigh from the line. Most everyone is busy with a phone, few if any evacuated without; exception Marcus, exception Sonja. Behind Sonja and Marcus is an elderly couple and a dozen other people. Twenty more in front of them. Marcus waves the couple ahead and they shuffle past. Sonja looks at Marcus. She guesses people are assuming they are a couple and wonders would that be a bad thing. In the line, nobody speaks unless into a phone. Some people sob. An employee distributes goody-bags and takes orders for drinks. Sonja orders a tall latte, Marcus orders three bottles of beer—any beer will do—and asks for a second goody bag. In each goody bag there is a chicken sandwich, an apple, and a Granola bar.

The line shortens. Sonja catches her reflection in the mirror behind reception and tries to fix her hair. She licks her fingers and wipes her smudged face. Marcus moves ahead and Sonja skips three steps to catch up. She takes his hand in hers. Marcus looks down, says What's this? She tells him she's in shock and needs comforting. Well that's okay then, says Marcus. A whisper comes down the line that there aren't enough rooms for everybody.

(The room which awaits them. The room has three Monet posters, two of which are the same. The curtains are heavy and dark, the carpet crimson. Whorish, the place feels whorish. There are two queen-sized beds in the room. Opposite the beds is a table and on the table sits a television. Beneath the table, a locked mini-bar. From the window, a smouldering hotel.)

Marcus pushing open the door. Marcus pushes the door and it swings heavily inward. Sonja stretches the toes of one foot over the threshold like she is testing the temperature of water. Then she is falling, then whooshing, as Marcus swoops her legs from beneath her. He advances into the room with Sonja in his arms. Her eyes are closed, as if she were on a fairground ride, her head tilted back. Sonja's hands join around Marcus' neck. Marcus bounces Sonja to a rest on the first bed. He runs his nose the length of her neck, from behind an ear to the nape. Sonja smells of burnt. There is a moment they share, in which to both it is clear what is coming. Another moment is upon them.

Four light knocks on the door, a slight pause between each knock. As if the knocker is trying to detect sound within. Marcus and Sonja look at each other like they have been discovered. Sonja opens her eyes wide; Marcus grimaces through clenched teeth. They rise from the bed together. Sonja goes to the bathroom; she half closes the door; she stands behind the door in darkness. Marcus clears his throat and says, Who's there? Room Service, comes the answer. Through the spy-hole Marcus sees an hotel employee holding a tray. A coffee and three beers. Marcus opens and takes the tray. Tonight there will be no tip. On the house, says the hotel employee, If there's anything else just ring down. Marcus asks if there is news of casualties. Two dead, two critical. The men are silent then and Marcus closes the door. The water starts in the bathroom, Won't be long, just taking a bath. The door is ajar and Marcus sees Sonja in the mirror. She has discarded her Miss Kitty pyjamas. Her hands hold the edge of the sink, she leans into the mirror and bites her lower lip, her eyes on Marcus. She has dark pink nipples, a triangle of light hair. Sonja smiles and bends to one side. I see you, she says. Coffee, says Marcus, and stretches his hand into the bathroom. He places the cup beside the sink.

Sonja takes a bath. Marcus twists open a beer and lies on the bed. Outside, the fire is defeated and the sky is dusty orange. Marcus sees the final spurts of water fall against the building. Fire-fighters call to each other, their voices full of work. Hose is coiled, ladders retracted, heavy red doors slam shut. The sirens sound again as each truck leaves the scene.

Marcus watches National Geographic. The new-born panda doesn't look like a panda, it looks like a fetus in a white fur coat. Rejected by its mother, the carer wraps the new-born in cashmere and places it in an incubator. The mother chews bamboo. Marcus learns that pandas are picky eaters—there are four hundred types of bamboo on the planet, of which pandas eat only three. They are eating, or not eating, themselves into extinction. After a month in the incubator the carer brings the fledgling back to the mother. She takes it with outstretched arms and retreats to a corner of the cubicle, where she turns her back to the world. The separation, and the show, is over. Marcus opens a second bottle and flicks off the TV. He lies back and drinks with closed eyes, Where is this going? he thinks. He hopes they salvaged his clothes, those jeans at least, he really liked those jeans. The bottle leans towards him, beer dribbles down his front. He wakes and puts the bottle aside. She's beautiful, he thinks. A quick shower when she's finished. Marcus sleeps.

Marcus sleeps, Sonja sleeps. The water is soft and quiet around her. The tips of her hair are wet and cold. Her mouth gapes wide. The inside of Sonja's mouth is a lighter shade of pink, as if red was rationed the day she was born. Beside her on the floor, the untouched coffee. Were Sonja awake she would revel at the quality of such a rare silence. There is nothing, nothing moves the air enough to make a sound.

Afternoon Performance

The static from the speaker pierces the afternoon. The clown behind the wheel stretches his arm out the window, drops a cigarette and fixes the aerial. He clears his throat and spits. More static, then *Come to the show.* See ferocious creatures; the most amazing … remarkable … unforgettable … Come to the show. We won't be back this way again. His voice doesn't convince. A seal balances a beach ball, applauds itself, does that deep-throat seal thing; a fat woman in a tutu holds a hula-hoop in the start position; clowns tease the strongman; a chimp in ring master attire throws sweets at onlookers, shrieks. The ringmaster, the actual ringmaster, twists his moustache and cracks his whip. People close enough remark on how the glint in his eye suggests he isn't all good. Rain starts to fall and the truck rolls on.

Un Sac Comme Le Mien

It's my bag, I'm one hundred percent sure it's my bag, but its contents are somebody else's. I check the name, my name, written in purple felt tip. My name. I am under no doubt that this is who I am. I look at my new student, sitting opposite, and smile. She's just arrived and this is our first meeting. Today's hour is to set goals, needs; break the ice. She picks up on the fact that I'm a little perturbed. Eh, I say, well. She smiles, leans forward. My English is not so good, she says. Well you're in the right place, I say, and look at the bag. I stand, put the bag on the table. My stuff must be in there, I root. No. I take out the stethoscope, put it on the table. We smile; she checks her watch. Somewhere, a doctor is attending a patient armed with Murphy's English Grammar in Use. So, tell me, I say, what are your expectations from this course? Expectations? Yes. She leans back, strokes her neck. Take a moment, I say, think about it. She nods, opens two buttons on her blouse. Would you like to? she says. To? She looks at the stethoscope. Ah, I say. She flicks her hair over her shoulders, holds her blouse open and fixes her gaze on the light fitting. I insert the rubber ends in my ears, the buds, and blow on the shiny part. I can do this, I've seen it done a thousand times. I walk around the table, bend and make contact. She shudders. I pull back. Sorry, cold? She smiles. I blow some more on the shiny part, rub it against the arm of my jacket. I bend. Now, breathe deeply. She does as directed. I bend closer. Her breasts rise to greet me. She smells of vanilla, perhaps a touch of cinnamon. I can see pores opening and closing, I think. I move the shiny part around, nod, say Hmm, and actually locate her heartbeat, northeast of the rim of her bra. I listen. Her heartbeat sounds like machine gun fire, spurts, then nothing, then again, then horses galloping across the sand, the bells of The Angelus, then—something I can make sense of—Morse. Dot, dash, dot-dot, dash. It comes fast and I write the letters on the table with a piece of red chalk: GRAMMAR. She stretches to see, I step back. I remove the buds from my ears, tell her she can button up. There's no point in being unprofessional. Well? she says, what? Nothing to worry about, I say, reassure her. Seems you have a grammar problem is all, nothing unusual in that. She nods, How serious? Too early to say, but let's not take any chances. I look at the bag, begin to root. Under the prescription pad, amongst the lotions, pills and potions, a jar of ointment catches my eye. The label reads Good for Grammer (sic). Rub gently into hands twice daily. This will do the trick, I say, and crack the seal. I take a gob, signal for her hand and begin to massage. The effect is instantaneous: she talks at length about herself; about her village on the Hungarian-Slovenian border; her pro bono stuff at the local arboretum; her membership of a Greco-Roman wrestling club. I smile, do that thing with my eyes. Maybe you can show me some moves? I say. Maybe we can trade? she answers. Sorry, strictly cash. She goes on, talks; point is, in the ten minutes or so that pass, she does not make one grammatical error. Living there all those years, she says (excellent use of the gerund employed as the subject of a sentence), I came to realise that, despite it being my home, I wouldn't reach my potential unless I—She withdraws her hand, offers the other in its place; I take another gob, apply. Please, I say, continue. I wonder how the doctor's getting on. There's a word, she says, what is it? A synonym for good, pleasant … agreeable. Hmm, I say. Agitation in her eyes. She withdraws her hand, fishes an electronic translator from her bag and taps some keys. Nice, she says. Pardon? The word I was looking for was *nice*, a new word for me. The penny drops, I realise with horror that the simplest vocabulary is dissolving. Nice, she says again, a, not difficult, what is the opposite of difficult? You mean *easy*? She taps some keys, Didn't know that one either. Perhaps I should listen to your heartbeat again? I say. Won't be necessary, she answers. It's clear that I am lacking very basic vocabulary. Hmm. I check the bag, find a bottle of pills marked "Elementary and Pre-Intermediate Vocab: allow one to dissolve under the tongue. Repeat as needed." Try one of these, I say. She does as directed then raps out a thousand words without drawing breath. Pills work. Oh, but how the pills work.

We have three minutes left on the clock. She leans forward. I want the bag, she says. No can do, say I. Give it fucking here, she says, moron. No deal, I say, not going to happen. I reach, she pounces. We struggle, fall to the ground. For a second we are as close to The Wheelbarrow Position as I have ever come. My concentration slackens, plummets, plunges. She shifts her weight and I am on the receiving end of The Boston Crab. I know a thing or two about wrestling, know I'm not leaving The Crab anytime soon. I breathe, everywhere hurts. To the side, periphery, the bag. Some pills have spilled on to the floor. They are tricolours, flags of the world. I hear a crack in my neck, feel it, wince. She squats beside me. I lie immobilised, her hand across my mouth. Parley the francey? she says, pushes pills into my mouth. They dissolve before I can spit. She stands, fixes her hair. I see her leave and cry for help, shadows. Il y a des gens autour de moi. Mon chef est là, quelques collègues et un monsieur que je ne connais pas. Il est medecin, j'en suis sûr. Il a l'air d'un médecin, de tout cas. Je ne comprendre pas ce qu'ils disent. Puis, je vois comment … je le regarde comme il ouvre son sac. Un sac comme le mien.

An Afternoon's Work

Things had been pretty slow around Antwerp, all this talk of major trading routes was horseshit. So I was scraping and scratching, doing the necessary to put crust on the table; nothing that would ever lift my name over the city's Gothic spires. I'd even put in a bid at the Rathuis for the cobbling of Grote Markt—the place was a mess of mud and shit and swill, far from what the burghers wanted for the city's main square—the future was definitely cobblestones. It was my first tender, my friend Walter did the paperwork, but we were undercut by a greasy Spaniard who reeked of oil and garlic. But what a job he did, he was a maestro. Still, what's the world coming to if a native loses out on work to a lowly immigrant. It should be a tocsin to us all.

Which brings me to the picture. Christmas was approaching, hand in hand with a dire need for monies, (not that there'd be gifts—the pox had long since taken my wife; the road my young—but still, ale isn't cheap.)

So, damnation, *malediction*; the picture; easy money.

Walter fixed it up. 'Just go there, pose, do as you are told.' It wasn't—at all—my line of work but a ducat is a ducat. Walter swore he'd keep it to himself, and besides, the kid, *l'artiste,* was a nobody. *Was.* Within a year the snot was being feted by kings and queens; fortunes were being exchanged for his canvases.

Though he used a woman in my place in subsequent versions of the picture, there was no mistaking my countenance in the original. I was a laughing stock. It just goes to show: we never know what lies around that next corner.

But back to then. He was no older than my youngest, studying the masters, building a portfolio, wooing patrons. He didn't seem the slightest interested in who we—myself and the other model—were. He didn't so much as introduce himself.

'You,' he said, 'Stand there,' and addressing the lady, 'You—disrobe.'

Well, I. My loins stirred as I watched her. She seemed unperturbed to discard her frock—and the rest—till finally she lowered the silk from her buttocks to her ankles. I felt more than I ever recall feeling, standing there fully clothed, beside this naked beauty. She was a sight, though probably not a lady. Her hair was held high by pins; her breasts were thick and portly. She followed my eyes following her curves to her slumbering schatz, then fixed me with raised eyebrows. I looked ahead. The kid stepped forward.

'So, get yourselves behind the sideboard. Eyes forward at all times, clear? Chin higher, just so. Now, you, finger and thumb, and yes—just so—hold her nipple, just enough pressure to keep it hard, firm at least.' Well … Whoever heard the likes. But I did as I was told, and pinched. She shrieked, and her breasts jumped and rolled, like young mammals at play. 'Try not to hurt her, man!' said, *exclaimed*, the kid, and I offered apologies. 'Let's try again,' he barked. So I reached across and took it. 'Easy,' she said—the only word she would ever say to me—in such a manner that I stiffened below.

'Perfect,' said the kid. 'And now to work.'

We stood and stood, stoney-faced and cold-eyed, then stood some more. It was the strangest pose but one never knows what's going through these modern artists' heads. I tweaked and tweaked for all I was worth, for three hours straight. I could feel her heart beating through her nipple, it quickened as the Cathedral's bell struck each quarter hour. I had to restrain myself from introducing the rest of my hand to her breast, though once—when the kid rose to close a window—I spat on my fingertips and tugged roughly: enough to make her suck air sharply; enough to tell me she knew I was there. My thoughts were scattered about her, thoughts which had little to do with nipples, and everything to do with the splaying of orifices. It was later, much later, when I picked up the change in her breathing, and when I dropped my eyes the reason presented itself in the shape of the three fingers inside her. Nice work, indeed. As much as I tried to fumble through my garments and free the beast below, I could not, not without releasing the nipple; not without attracting the kid's attention. I'd never before witnessed a scene of this kind, and I'd had my share of whores and even a witch once—a Moor who'd combusted into fire when I ejaculated across her sleeping nakedness. The nipple hardly needed my attention as the thrashing continued below. If *l'artiste* had registered the spectacle, he pretended otherwise. Then she slowed and stopped; from her throat the slightest yelp, then a cough, and I knew the game had reached its conclusion.

We were dismissed shortly thereafter with a curt, 'That will be all for today. Same time, same place, next Tuesday.' He did not so much as look up as we exited stage right. When we left the atelier and stepped into the afternoon light, we did so as strangers. There was no frivolous or wanton banter, nor were there pleasantries; no bodily fluids were exchanged. She turned to the left; I to the right, to the tavern. I drank a skin-full of ale that night. Walter didn't believe a word, not even when I showed him the imprint of her nipple, burned between my finger and thumb. I drank and sat and wondered what Tuesday might bring.

The Water Carrier

Alabaster rump, armless since antiquity, I wrapped her in a sheet and took her home. Athena of Macedonia, the nameplate said. The plan, the original plan, was to point out holes in their security, then sign them up for a makeover: CCTV, movement sensors, three-minute armed response unit; business had gone south and I was resorting to whatever it takes to save my business. S'funny how resort and *resort to* are worlds apart on the continuum of well-being.

At home I laid her out on the couch and considered what a beauty she must have been. I cranked up the heat and poured myself three fingers. It had been a long day and I lay down beside her—not perving or anything, just wanting to crash awhile. I ignored the first shiver, not long after, thought I was already under. But a second followed and I was alert, then a third, fourth and fifth and I pulled back the sheet in time to see her breathe her first.

After three days she'd thawed to the point that I thought sex might be feasible, but every time I got cosy she threatened me with plagues of stuff I didn't know existed. She asked where my slaves were; where I kept the small boys—she was learning English, fast, from the History Channel. That Helen was such a tramp. Hector? This small. Achilles? *Please.* Pass the grapes, will you?

The museum and the cops were winding down their investigation. Eastern Europeans, they told the papers, were the most probable culprits, for a private collector; that or students, a prank. She anyway wasn't that special, they said, probably a water carrier, a servant of some kind; they'd mixed up the nameplates. I never told her. If I got my pitch right and landed the contract, and stayed on her good side, there was no saying where this could go.

Mooring

We moored at the mouth of the fjord, the weekend the clocks changed. It was a wet one, squalls. Wind rain wind rain. We pulled on our oilskins and braced ourselves.
"A bit blowey," she said, shouted. "A bit," I shouted back.

~

We stuck it out till the light faded; a kind of sunset without sun. Below, we turned on the space heater and stripped off.

~

"I'll need you here early on Monday," he'd said down the phone. "I'll need to get you up to speed; you'll need to hit the ground running."

~

I thought hard about his verbs.

~

We'd had a good run and couldn't complain. Our supplies were out but we'd managed—the ocean had provided. We scraped cockles from the rocks that Sunday. We fried them in oil and seasoned them with white pepper. She pulled a couple of Heinekens out of nowhere, said *Da-daah*.

~

Monday arrives, its silence wakes us; not a breeze not a wave not a gull. I dress, good to go.

~

Spring forward; Fall back.

~

She pecks me on the cheek, a symbol from this other world.
"I'll be here," she says

~

I find the stop and take the bus. The bus follows the telephone wires. The city sucks me back to Present Tense. It grows in the window until I am small.

Cyclicismus

We swept the leaves and piled them high. The pile didn't block the sun or anything, but it took a half minute to circumnavigate. We used a battery-powered soup blender to reduce the leaves to chips, then granulate, then powder. We added water from the lake and two sacks of cement. Other stuff got mixed in: bugs, hair, dirt, cigarette butts and at least one dead field mouse. We used a shoebox as a mould, slapped in the pulp with a rusted trowel. It took three days for the bricks to dry. Winter at the door, we started laying brick. With a little imagination, the pile that had been leaves started to resemble a leafy yurt, vaguely.

Things hadn't worked out at our previous addresses. There'd been a squat in Camden Town, a flat-share in Berlin and a Christmas on the streets. There'd been a neurotic great aunt on Rhode Island. Don't know what we were thinking. There was the bivouac in The Adirondacks. We'd liked it there, until the weather changed and the bears moved us on. So we walked south, into Fall. Winter never far behind. We traveled light—apart from our yearbooks, my mother's cookbook, and the twelve hundred page printout of the family tree; stuff we burned to keep us warm. We watched my ancestors rise in the smoke. Comes a time to let go. The paper gone, we spooned to stay warm.

The bricks rise with the days. The sky says snow. On a Wednesday, a fat man with square glasses stops by from the Buildings and Planning Authority. He gets out of his car, says, 'The hell are you kids doing?′ His voice is octaves above where he'd probably want it to be. He places his briefcase on a stack of bricks, sits on it and crosses his legs; tries to cross his legs, it doesn't work and they fall apart. He is too fat to cross anything. His hands haven't seen each other since he was a lad. But he's beautiful like a Botero is beautiful. We tell him so, 'You're beautiful, beautiful, beautiful, beautiful, beautiful, beautiful, beautiful.' We could go on but he waves for us to stop. We quiet down. 'So,' he says. He lights a long thin cigarette, blows out the match and drops it at his feet. 'So. Let's take a look at this baby.'

Shore Leave

First came Dublin, porter and rain; longshoremen and short-arsed chancers. Everyone drunk and not giving a damn—feckless, they called it—a breath away from losing grip. The Gulf Stream thick with ballads and profanity. Then came Antwerp, fierce proud Flemish eyes; botched tattoos lauding big ships and mother. Everyone drunk and not giving a damn. A stevedore told us that all ports were so, that that was why men went to sea; to put in at port and not give a damn. We drank to that and much more else, woke rank and wanting more—ate onions, spuds, horsemeat with brown mustard; ale after ale after ale. Up the coast around the Hook, Rotterdam. The same strain in every eye—drunk, not giving a Dutch damn. Herring, they said, steels the gut for beer soak. We ate their herring and drank their brew, sang shanty after shanty. *Home boys home.* A breath away from losing grip. Thick tongued and ropey, two days to reach Cuxhafen. We toasted Kaiser Bill and Lorelei, dead German poets we'd never read. (The locals said we talked in clichés, but offered no alternatives.) The night stretched, the outcome as before, in Dublin and Antwerp and Rotterdam. The Cuxhafeners told us they'd visit, if ever we found home. They told us to avoid Norwegian whalers. They told us—warned and convinced us—not to go to Hamburg, for the beer was sour and the women there had no teeth. They told us to continue north to Greenland, to the ports of Sisimiut and Paamiut, that we would be welcomed there. They told us they'd remember us, that they'd sing our names in song.

Out of Landshut

I thought about what the envelope might hold, and the mood it might give rise to. The return name and address read Frederick Manuel of Landshut. The writing was thick and looped and all too decorative for my liking. The stamp (first class postage) celebrated a seventeenth century Viennese wheelwright, of whom I'd also never heard. He had a thick gut and an eye patch. I pulled up a chair and rolled one cigarette after the other until I had enough for the day and started smoking my way forward. Manuel, I thought, Frederick Manuel of Landshut. What news out of Landshut could possibly concern me? My mind wandered—I thought of Landshut's proximity to München, and a Sauerbraten I had eaten there when I was still an enlisted man. I remembered the lisping etymology professor at the next table, and the waiter with the red sideburns. Who was this Frederick Manuel? What could he want? Did he represent others, perhaps? And if so, who? I feared, I admit, the unleashing of the unknown. I made fresh coffee and stoked the fire. ... Later, when the postman passed by at the end of his shift, I gave him the letter and advised him to return it. Nothing in Landshut was of any concern to me. The postman tucked the letter inside his coat and continued on his way. There was not much left of the day, not enough to begin anything worthwhile, so I smoked my last cigarette and watched the fire die.

At the Neuwiener Hütte

We picked up the pace when the hut came into view; our tongues thick with thoughts of Hefeweizen. We left our packs outside, as instructed by a sign over the door, and entered. It would be a short stay; we wanted the summit—and to pitch our tents—before nightfall. Inside was dark, though not so dark as the Wirt, a sour man who didn't greet us, who didn't so much as nod when we ordered the beer. And we his only guests, it seemed. His mood could not dull ours, however, and thoughts of the peak. The beer was good and the banter fast. We spoke of climbs in years gone by, of midgey-infested landscapes and of who'd snored loudest. Then a lull, and a voice from the corner—in a dialect of Tyrolean that none of us knew. The man, thick-boned and hirsute—eyebrows like moustaches—had one green eye and one, perhaps diseased, yellow. His nose a twisted olive branch. A stein of beer and a blue-brown hunk of cheese sat untouched in front of him as he spoke. And spoke. We gestured that we did not understand and he started over, this time in Italian, of which we knew less. The Wirt brought more beer, but ignored our requests for translation. Someone said the man smelled of goat, though the smell may have been sheep or poultry for all we knew; still, The Goatherd was the name we gave him. He extended a black finger and drew figures in the air, which proved futile, for each of us saw—and called out—something different—Dog! Cat! Drowned goat! Four-legged horned or winged creature! until finally we agreed that the man's donkey lay lame at the bottom of a gully, two days' walk away. The Goatherd wanted us to accompany him and rescue the beast—we thought, our interpretation conjecture at best. The Wirt brought beer. We explained our plans as best we could, and The Goatherd stroked his brow, and raised the black finger again, Cat! Dog! Goat! we called. Someone shushed, said *The summit*—if we don't go now, nothing more, and we stood to leave. We wished The Goatherd and his donkey well. He answered with more signs—a storm was coming, a bad one, and we should stay the night. We supposed this a ruse. We asked the Wirt to explain that nightfall stalls for no man, and this time he opened his mouth as if to speak, and revealed the empty cave behind his lips—the man had neither tongue nor teeth. We spun to the door and filed out, wanting to leave this place for good; the sky barked and darkened, then howled as if in pain. The first rain fell, silent globules big as eyes. We looked back to the entrance of the hut; the door was closed, but from behind it came laughter.

Out of Kitzbühel

Orla's Ethics professor starved himself to death; her brother cycled off a cliff. The cantor climbed the church's steeple and stepped into the air. All in the wake of Orla's death. Her father hung himself in the forest outside Kitzbühel; her sister cut her own throat. A neighbour was next, then a cousin then a colleague then the baker from whom Orla had bought an almond croissant every day for fifteen years.

The town council watched, sure that they were witnessing a suicide pact, unsure of how to stop it. When the mayor self-immolated, the council appointed an investigating constable, Idstein, and told him to find out What and Why, at the double, and put his findings in a report.

The Very Reverend Monsignor O'Brien, having buried eighteen of Kitzbühel's suicides, stepped in front of the regional train to Innsbruck.

Kitzbühel; bedecked with wreaths and sprays of lilies.

Orla, for the record, had drunk Obstler until her liver hung over her belt and people thought she had a puppy under her shirt. She didn't care for life, she liked to say. Orla Steinbach drank herself to death.

A month passed; with each new day a suicide.

Idstein was no nearer to determining What and Why. When asked by the town council about his progress, he suggested they exhume Orla's body and extract her brain. They should send the brain to Innsbruck for tests. In Innsbruck they would know What and Why. Or perhaps Vienna. In Vienna they would know for sure.

And so Orla's body was exhumed and her brain extracted. The responsible surgeon said it quite smelled of almonds.

The brain was placed in a large glass jar and filled with alcohol. It was packaged for transit and brought to the postmaster by members of the town council, of which there remained three. The postmaster licked then applied the requisite value of stamps to the package, and assured the council that it would be sent that afternoon, that it would arrive in Innsbruck the following morning. Content with proceedings, the town council members withdrew to Uli's Gasthaus and ordered Spätzle with fried onions and glass after glass of Landwein.

The package was lost in transit.

The postmaster drown himself in the pond at Gieringer Weiher. His wife climbed over the tiger enclosure at Kitzbühel's Zoologischer Garten. Their son thrust wet hands into the unlocked armature of an electricity pylon.

In Idstein's report, which was unfinished, he claimed the suicides would end. All those who had committed suicide had done so in different manners. There would only be as many suicides as there were ways to commit suicide. Then Idstein disemboweled himself on the steps of the Bäckerei. The remaining burghers of Kitzbühel packed their belongings, intent on leaving. But none of them succeeded, and the suicides continued.

Invisible Man

The days rolled over Ray with a sameness that numbed his nuts and froze any semblance of fantasy he ever may have known. Uninvited images arrived before his eyes with increasing frequency, frames from a movie he'd seen—about an artist who awoke in the picture he'd painted. Spam, thought Ray.

The sameness that polluted Ray could be seen in the choices he made—at the canteen; in the way he dressed; in the sites he cruised and in the TV he watched. The sameness could be seen in Ray's penchant for slasher movies and the three cans of Bass he lowered down his gullet each and every evening. Same same same.

Then.

Ray would recall that it was a Wednesday and he'd just stepped out of the shower. He stretched, and yawned across the steam-filled bathroom in the direction of the mirror. When his reflection didn't respond, didn't seem to respond, Ray thought Condensation and raised his hand and began to wipe. His chest and shoulders showed themselves, same, definitely his. There; his reflection wasn't wiping, its hands gripped the edge of the sink. Pulse boomed in Ray's ears. He exhaled, squinted and peered into the mirror; the reflection was wide-eyed, wide- and wild-eyed. It folded its arms.

Ray backed into the hallway. He touched his brow, ran his hands along his limbs, stared at his palms. There was nothing untoward, nothing odd or noteworthy. Except. He arched his neck around the frame of the bathroom door, his reflection leaned forward.

Ray turned and walked to the bedroom, calmly, each step echoed the crash of the pulse in his neck, in his head. He opened the wardrobe. The mirror inside the door reflected the wall behind him. Ray dressed, he didn't miss a button. He didn't need a mirror to fix his tie. He tied his shoes and took his overcoat from the stand in the hall. He lay the overcoat across his arm, paused, turned to the front door, then to the bathroom door and back and forth, and back again. This continued for a minute perhaps, perhaps two. Ray arched his neck around the bathroom door again—still there, still very much there, head bowed now so that the eyes were not visible, still there. A wisp of smoke, or steam perhaps, had appeared at a nostril. The face darted up, startled, the eyes swam on crimson lakes. Its complexion had paled to pewter.

Ray had no time for this, for whatever this was. There was a timetable that wouldn't wait for him and if he didn't leave n-o-w, a train would pull away from St Margaret's without him and a connection would be missed at Liverpool Street and, well, it didn't bear thinking about, the sequence of events that might follow. Ray stood in front of the door and lifted his hand to the bolt.

The Soundtrack of My Life

I was surprised that my ad caught his eye but there he was in the hallway with his piano. Man, but you are going to love this one, he said, and started to play. He was right, love it I did. Let's get you inside, I said, but his only reply was to play on. So I stepped out and pushed the piano and adjoined piano stool, upon which sat Thelonius Monk, into my apartment; his concentration unbroken. And so it began. No one would, could or will ever play like him, and every last note had a place in the soundtrack to my life. The job's yours, I told him, and I'm honored, for the record. He cracked a smile but didn't look up from the zone. I called the paper and told them to pull the ad—the position was filled, and oh but how.

I brought him tea or nibbles every few hours, whatever was going, and even then Monk did not stop, but played on with one hand while he drank, while he ate; notes drenched in heart. Days passed, weeks. If he used the bathroom it was when I stepped out on errands. He was busy with the soundtrack and nothing but. Deep in the night I'd feel the mattress depress and Monk would join me in bed. And when I woke it was to music. You're going to love this one, he'd call over; it was like those were his favourite words. Certainly, they became mine.

My life and its soundtrack, however, were larger than the confines of my apartment, so I hired a crew to push Monk and his piano around my world—five Estonian navvies and a little guy who said he'd been a cox at Cambridge. They negotiated the streets, the traffic, never more than three steps behind me; they owned the underground. Their chaperonage was silent and love-struck, inspired by Monk and his sais-pas-quoi. People would stop and point, say, Hey, eh, isn't that Monk? Is he writing the soundtrack to your life or something? And I'd say Yes, that is exactly what is going down here.

Word spread like a rash and people started to follow us—of course for the soundtrack, but some just to see what headwear

Monk was wearing on any given day. Some tried to ingratiate themselves into his presence with chit-chat and flattery, but no chance, the master's concentration stayed unbroken. Concerned, though, that he would be distracted, I decided to take precautions, and stopped by a Four Seasons to ask the concierge if he might give, loan or sell me a Do Not Disturb sign or two. I will never forget the look on that man's face, how his mouth made the most perfect, beautiful O as Monk played in the lobby. A bellboy said we should try Housekeeping, and was kind enough to make a call, but no one picked up—it was tools down when Monk came to town. Had the internet existed back then, well, I hate to think about the circus that would have developed. Al Gore, however, was still a very small boy.

The logistics of getting from A to B—where A was home and B was the bar, beach or bookshop—was not easy with the droves that followed us, and the other droves that camped outside my building. After I disconnected the bell and the phone, they pushed notes under my door and filled the mailbox with requests for interviews, love, and to jam with Monk. I read some of them to him and he said Man, if you are cool with troubadours, fine—but charge them for the privilege of contributing to the soundtrack of your life. So I did, fifty bucks per quarter hour. The line went three blocks west. Mostly they played stoned caterwaul, but I indulged them because lives and their soundtracks, I guess, have interludes that don't seem to belong, or only do so in retrospect, if at all. I was happy living life in this manner, happier still with my soundtrack. Fine as long as Monk was fine—he seemed so—though I doubted at times. Are you happy, Monk? I'd say, and he'd cackle and shake his head, maybe shush me. He wasn't big with words, he didn't need to be. And somehow down the years I became a little like him, a little Monk by default, in that I didn't say much anymore. There were times I wanted to ask him stuff, sure, like what was with the Countess?, and I'd wait for an interval, but intervals were as frequent as buses during the holidays. And, when one did come along, my questions felt trite. The man was his music and nothing else mattered.

Monk's eyes were faraway planets. Years had passed, so many I'd lost count; I was bedridden, beyond ailing, and oblivion was just breaths away. Around the room, the navvies, the little cox guy, all quiet. The soundtrack of my life now accompanied by the drone of a nebulizer. Monk hadn't aged, nor had his playing, it was more relevant and vital than ever. Then our eyes met, and I knew that the music, the waves I was hearing, was my finale; to which my eyelids slowly fell.

The Small Boy and The Big Cat

It was a playground like any other, apart from the tiger in the linden tree. There were swings and a slide, a roundabout and monkey bars. And there was a *schaukel-korb*, a swinging basket big enough for a small family to lie back in. It was from there that the tiger came to our attention. Joshua and I were schaukeling to and fro, schaukeling and singing our new song, which was one line, 'Flieeeeegen, wie ein Vooooooogel,' to and fro and back and forth. Fly Like a Bird. At thirty months, Joshua didn't have all his basic phonemes downs, but his V was coming on fine; we schaukeled and sang our line, content in the afternoon.

Joshua stopped singing.

I looked over and saw that he was staring on high, into the branches of the linden, one hand raised. He looked at me and said,

'Tigger.'

Tigger: as in the German pronunciation for tiger. I laughed and called him a crazy little man, he frowned in reply, scrunched deep and punched his hand higher.

'Tigger,' he said, louder this time. 'Yeah, yeah,' I said, 'A tigger in the linden, sure. And a hefelump on the slide?' Too much TV, I thought, or too much Milne. (Could a kid get too much Milne?) But I looked up and sure enough—between the branches and the leaves, up high and all but out of view—was a tiger. I froze. A tiger; not a metaphor for something weird—a regular, card-carrying tiger, and it was moving south, in our direction. Unusual in these parts, downtown Frankfurt. Joshua, having lost interest in our song, sat up in the schaukel-korb.

'TIGGER!!!' he screamed. Even one so young knew these were exceptional goings-on.

The parents and offspring in the vicinity looked over. The parents gave indulgent smiles; the kids united in the universal hysterics of panic: screaming and running in aimless circles. Cries of Tigger! Tigger! Tigger! were punctuated with cries of Papapapapapa. Two minutes later the dust had settled from the fleeing kiddy-wagons and we were alone. I wondered, worried even, why my adrenalin hadn't engaged. The tiger lowered itself from branch to branch to branch, pirouetted 360, then plopped into the schaukel-korb. Well, now. I'd read reports, way back, somewhat conflicting reports, about how to act when confronted by a bear—make yourself big, make yourself small, run—but tigers, this was whole new territory, so I did what came naturally: made space. Joshua squealed a squeal that knew no fear. Then he squealed another and threw himself at the tiger, pulled hard on its whiskers and did his best tiger roooaaaaaarrrr. I've never seen a tiger laugh and I'm not one hundred per cent sure that's what it was—the rumble from deep, the contracting and loosening abdomen—but one thing was sure, he (she? it?) wasn't objecting. Let's say it was a male—he held up a paw and with a swoosh, knocked Joshua out of the korb and into the sandpit below. He joined him with a bounce and the two of them rolled around, Joshua pulling fur and biting the tiger's face.

'Easy, tiger,' I said from the korb and sat up in slow-mo. If either of them heard me, they didn't let on. Whatever possessed Joshua to push the crown of his skull into the beast's mouth is beyond me. I cringed and looked away, 'Joshua, *nein*,' I hissed and caught the tiger's eye, which didn't seem especially pleased. I lay back in the korb and bit my fist. When I dared look again, Joshua was on the tiger's back. He held himself steady via handfuls of whisker and they took off, jumping over swings, up and down the slide. It was a sight like none I'd known. I wished I'd brought the camera or invested in a fancy-dan phone. Joshua specially enjoyed the slide and shouted 'Nochmal, Tigger, nochmal!' and the tiger obliged and round they went again, Joshua clinging to his ears.

The sound of sirens. The tiger looked up; he knew. He looked proud and fierce and sad. He bucked his rear and Joshua was airborne and squealing again. The tiger softened his fall with a paw and ran his tongue across his face; Joshua punched him in the eye. The tiger crouched and stretched and yawned. Only now did I note the claws, longer and thicker than Joshua's fingers. In one leap he was above us and in the linden, up and into the airy heights. The last branch gave way and leaned into the street; he leapt again and reached a roof. He pulled his weight over the apex and bounced away, disappearing over rooftops, into the late afternoon. The police and fire engines and ambulances screeched to a halt. The police drew their weapons and rushed around the perimeter of the playground. They shouted 'Keine Bewebung,' like they meant it, but we weren't going anywhere, we were back in the schaukel-korb, schaukeling to and fro, trying to remember the melody to our song.

The line for coffee

resembled ∞

;

I couldn't but dwell

and glory in the shuffle.

A Day Much Like Another

I bob and weave my way through, deftly side-stepping a box of Barbie bodyparts. Who are these people and what are they doing in my park? Tattoo convention? guys with tribal shoulders, girls in short-short tops showing love-handles and sexy tattooed lower backs. Their offspring: dozens, hundreds maybe, their tattoos washawayable, scrambling for the best spots around the perimeter of the wide open lawn, miscellaneous currency signs in their eyes. I remember—it's the day before school starts over—when the local kids have their flea market. Boxes, bags, tables, and shoes and clothes and toys. An assault course of childhood paraphernalia. I zip by.

Today's special at The Park Café is Greek yoghurt with honey, topped with crushed almonds, €3.99. Maybe later, right now I'm running, exercising-exorcising, sprinting past a couple of junkies sparking and inhaling. The bell from the Dutch Reformist Church strikes the hour. A dozen Asians converse beside the swings. Indians or Pakistanis, I don't know, play cricket. I wonder how they stand on Kashmir. Africans play football, soccer, if you're reading this in the U. S. of A. A Dalmatian shits in the fountain. Few joggers today, Nordic walkers though—four abreast—taking up space, making a racket with their ski-poles, yakking their heads off. A dead mouse, on its back, looking all cartoon-like. More prams and strollers heading to the flea market—stern young fathers, an attractive young mother throws a last-second sideways glance. You bet I would. Man, but was I bad last night. Couple more corners, pulse normal, some sweat on brow. Older silent couple on a bench, staring off into the trees. He's thinking about pussy, I know he is; she's thinking about the grandkids. A canary bikini, inhabited by someone I'd like to rub down, olive skin, jet black hair. She lies on her stomach and I can't see her face. But sometimes a guy just knows.

The junkies are flaked out in the bushes. Sirens from the street. I'm not ratting on anyone. Pulse circa 160. My nipples sting, forgot to apply the damn Vaseline, again. A mobile bratwurst unit takes up position in the centre of the lawn. A kid screams and kicks the air as his mother sells Winnie the Pooh. But honey you said you didn't want Winnie anymore. Other kids giggle; the a-m Dalmatian receives a slap to the head; a cat chomps down the dead mouse and slinks away, swinging its head from side to side. Mixing my drinks was not a good idea—all that beer followed by ouzo, followed by gin when they ran out of ouzo—not good. The Asians play football with the Africans. The canary bikini sits upright, her back like Dali's Gala. She has a luminous green band in her hair, and matching glittzery earrings. HOWZAT? roars the cricket crowd, and turn to face the umpire, because that's what they do when someone's been caught out. Pulse, 178.

The Talk Test—run, but only fast enough that you can hold a normal conversation. You asshole, get out of here! How could you? I never want to see you again. I mean it this time. Go! So I made a pass at her sister. Let her cool off, take a bath, everything will work out. Blame booze; promise abstinence. A woodpecker smacks its head into/against a tree; a frisbee whizzes past, having the time of its life; cricketeers clap politely. The junkies are up again, running around and screaming their heads off, looking for Anton. Anton, if you read this, stay the fuck away from the park. The kid has his Pooh-bear back and nurses it in his arms. His mother scowls. A jogger with the Nike logo tattooed on her shoulder. Why on earth would anyone do such a thing? Twelve grim faces in the line for bratwurst, like a jury waiting for evidence. And a tattooed dragon breathing crimson fire at the sword-wielding portrait of the guy whose skin it is on. He's gained a few pounds since the tattoo was done, and lost a lot of hair. There are similarities to the cover a Meatloaf albums. I wonder how that works with copyright infringement. My sweat tastes of beer. The football game is all go. Their women look on, and stoke the barbecue. Canary bikini is resting her back against a tree, book in lap, hair hides her face. I wonder would she want me too. They never do, they just want to be my friend. The cat purrs from the shade. I can change, I can change. But not now; not yet; maybe not ever.

Slight pain left knee, probably nothing to worry about. Junkies being pursued by police on horseback. The flea market kids scream in delight, except two—maybe six years between them—who are pissing against the church and checking out each other's wiener. Mothers busy with phones. I'm sweat-soaked through, ouch, Jogger's Nipple, stinging secretions. Damn Vaseline. I negotiate the flea market quicker than I'd prefer but the decibels are too much, every table-blanket-stall, blasts a different music. Crack of a cricket bat, such a beautiful sound. Incline, pulse 185. She's lying on her side now, and a lot of bikini is gathered in the crack of her ass. Cat sleeps with one eye, eyes a group of pigeons with the other. People pass by, phones in hand.

Left nipple bleeding slightly. A bell strikes the hour. I cut a couple of corners, by-passing the market, the football, the café. She's on the phone now, to her mother or a girlfriend, telling how I disgraced myself again, and how this time she means it for real. Again. The Africans cheer a goal. A woman sprays beer across the barbecue. I pass through a cloud of meaty fumes. No change at the bikini station. The cat moves like a leopard to where the pigeons are feeding.

The Love Song of H.R.K. Sommers

To say that I failed to find favour with the city's editors gave rise to a question from the rancid depths of rejection: How badly had I failed? I needed to know. The question—the putrid, stinking question—consumed and immobilised me. All four hundred eleven city editors had rejected my submission, and not one of those rejections was personalised. So, clearly, I'd failed with a certain *sais-pas-quoi*. But how badly? Despairingly? Pathetically? Adverbs swam around my head, flipping over and out of sight like screensaver dolphins.

So I called them—all four hundred eleven editors—and got every last one of their voicemails. I left my message—the message that would become *the* message—'This is H.R.K. Sommers. How badly did I fail?' (I used the pseudonym so as not to confuse authorship of this submission with others which carried my actual name or one of my other pseudonyms.) Every reiteration of the message down every telephone line was fuel on the fire of my desire for knowledge, and the fire grew—that baby blazed. My desire for knowledge became a campaign; it morphed in the night from Tuesday to Wednesday, whereupon phase two, email, began. 'This is H.R.K. Sommers, ' I wrote. 'How badly did I fail?' One reply arrived almost immediately, from the editor at Big City Quarterly Review. He would be out of his office until the seventeenth and any urgent business should be addressed to his assistant, a certain *taub* AT bcqreview DOT com. I redirected and sat in wait. And sat in wait. And. Bored, I googled *taub*, and found that it means *deaf* in German. How very *drole*. By three p.m. no other replies had arrived; by five, two. Both of them adverbs: 'Badly,' read the first and 'Badly, ' read the second. I wondered had they conferred. No more replies arrived, not on Wednesday and not on Thursday when I began phase three of the campaign and rented the office building opposite City Editor Central and painted the message, letter by letter, in the building's windows. I went with upper case, each about three feet square, over two floors. 'THIS IS H.R.K. SOMMERS: HOW BADLY DID I FAIL? ' I'd finished painting before I realised I should have written back-to-front but I'm sure they understood, being editors and all. My actions attracted attention from the street and onlookers stood and pointed, but I felt like the guy trying to show people the moon and all they can see is a finger, pointing. Not one city editor appeared at the windows of City Editor Central. Blinds shuffled here and there, but not enough to suggest it was orchestrated. It was like they didn't care. Nobody left the building through the front exit. I thought hard about phases four, five and six of the campaign. I needed to know.

'This is H.R.K. Sommers. How badly did I fail?' read the full-page ads in the next morning's papers. A couple more mails trickled in: 'Awfully,' 'Horribly' and 'Excruciatingly,' but the numbers weren't enough to suggest any type of consensus. I could sit and wait for more replies but there was so much to do, and I was going to need back-up. I called Manpower and they sent over Rick and Janine. By two that afternoon I had briefed them in full. These weren't kids just along for the ride, they took notes and asked questions, nodded and made good eye contact. And then they got stuck in. They had the T-shirts ready by five—ten thousand of them—and, by six, an army of volunteers mobilised to distribute them to rush-hour commuters. 'This is H.R.K. Sommers,' read the T's, 'How badly did I fail?' 'Dreadfully,' read the latest mail. Four hundred four city editors had still not replied, or was it four hundred three? Rick ran up an Excel sheet, it was vital that we get our numbers right. U2 arrived in our War Room just after six, unexpected but made welcome by all present. We were being heard, no doubt about it, but—frankly—I had to check my cynicism, concerned as I was that they would steal our thunder, that they would be a distraction, that Larry would hit on Jan, that Bobo wouldn't quit reciting the Beckett thing. In their defence, I have to say, the defining moment of the campaign became their impromptu rooftop concert. Their rendition of Satisfaction teared me up. Light aircraft circled overhead, banners trailing behind (Rick's idea). The banners read, well, the message hadn't changed. We were headline news at eight. Larry King called and I gave my first interview. 'What message do you want to send to the city editors?' he said. That guy cracks me up. I had Charley Rose on two and Letterman on three.

The campaign spilled over the borders that night. While we slept, demonstrators took to the streets of Seoul and Melbourne. In New Zealand a sheep farmer sprayed his flock with the message and even if they wouldn't stay in line it was pretty clear what was going on. Kind of. News came over the wire that French rail workers were striking in sympathy. We marched on Government Buildings on Friday. People cared, people wanted to know. How badly? Responses continued to trickle: 'Desperately,' 'Outrageously,' 'Pompously,' 'Despairingly (x4).' Only a fool could fail to see the trend but trends are sometimes misleading—and often inconclusive. I hired a statistician and more kids from Manpower; I hired a web guy, a Web 2.0 savvy dude who spoke in code. In Berlin, an estimated two hundred thousand punks, hippies and whores and took to the streets—the pictures of them stripped at Checkpoint Charlie would go on to win a Pulitzer. But somehow I wasn't sure if the message was translating as it should. The responses trickled some more and we put the results on the Web for all to see. Transparency was hip, it was the 21st century. My favourite response—if we can talk about favourite adverbs—the one I least despised and thought best surmised how badly I'd failed was… 'Exquisitely.' Failing exquisitely was failing with cojones, in H.R.K. Sommers' book.

That weekend, true, things slowed. It was becoming difficult to carry through on the gravitas we'd grown, to find a next level. The French rail workers striked again, which was nice, but with it being weekend maybe fewer people noticed. In England, Manchester United played Chelsea on Saturday evening and the players stood around the centre circle in a minute's silence, but a lot of people weren't sure why. The War Room was slow—Jan hadn't showed in a couple of days, and wasn't taking her phone. People started talking about Oscars and Super Bowls and—if ever we needed confirmation that the campaign was faltering—people started discussing *The Economy*. Rick zapped through the TV: we were nowhere, not a mention. City editors' responses had crawled to a halt; seventy four. I heard whispers, 'What now?' but only that, whispers. I considered resending the submission and discussed the implications with Rick. Maybe use another pseudonym. By this time a lot of the world was in Sunday afternoon and that's exactly how the campaign felt. Of the three diehard campaign workers who hadn't returned to their lives, only Rick wasn't doing Sudoku. I wasn't sure what to do next. I thought about washing the windows, admitted to myself that that was maybe the thing to do—move on—to start the cleansing. I ran some water into a bucket, started looking for rags. Dish soap.

Then it happened—the phone rang. I picked up. Dalaifucking-Lama. Or some guy who said that's what he was. His accent though, was really, really good. 'What now?' he said. 'People still want to know. They need to know. It's their nature, it is the human condition.' He said other stuff about Sam and Sara that went right over my head. And I was distracted by the phones which had begun to ring again—slow and intermittent, then hopping, and there weren't enough ears to take all the messages of support. The whisper roared: 'WHAT NOW?' I felt something new inside, smelt something new—my fingers itched for a pencil, a story was coming on. Rick and I withdrew to my office, closed the door. We ordered Chinese and I opened up a legal pad. It was going to be a long night.

Frank Joins The Dots

Frank's career in improv didn't pan out. There'd been a couple of gigs, sure, and there was always open-mic, but probably he shouldn't have quit the bank. He saw that now.

Fine. Apart from the bills. The bills worried Frank. But everything happens for a reason and everything's connected, Frank—actually—believed. He just had to join the dots. Frank trusted the dots, and trusted that they'd materialise any day now. When the time was right. Any. Day. Now. The dots would guide him.

Frank shows his mean face and waves a couple of fingers over his head, a cocked thumb. 'Everybody be cool. This is a robbery!' People hit the floor. Easy, thinks Frank, so fucking easy. This is Frank's first bank job. He lowers his faux pistol, but keeps it cocked. He winds his way through bodies, apologises when he steps on a hand.

At the counter, Gloria says 'Jeez, Frank, bad career move.'

'It's my first,' says Frank.

'You know, I thought that.'

'How am I doing?'

'Well, apart from hitting a bank you used to work at? Maybe a mask?'

Frank looks down, nods. He pinches the skin between his chin and throat. 'So,' he says.

'Yeah, anyway,' says Gloria.

'We should probably, you know … '

'Yeah,' says Gloria, 'let's do this. You got a bag?'

Frank frowns.

'You didn't bring a bag?'

'I left it in the car.'

Gloria sighs. 'But you got an actual real-life car, right?'

Frank doesn't answer.

'Let me see what I got here,' says Gloria. She fills an Aldi bag with used fives, tens and twenties. She throws in a couple of fifties for old times' sake, hands the bag to Frank.

'You should probably get going. The cops, you know.'

'Yeah. Much obliged, Gloria. Say hi to Hal.'

'You take care, Frank.'

Frank tips a hat that isn't there, turns and exits.

Outside, sirens. Police cars screech to a halt. Just like the movies, thinks Frank. He holds an imaginary hostage in a stranglehold, two fingers to an invisible head.

TV guys film from the end of the street.

'Nobody moves or she gets it,' shouts Frank. 'Don't say I didn't warn you muthas.' Thick moustachioed cops look back and forth, shrug, a SWAT team takes up position. Frank paces left then right.

'Don't make me do it!' he shouts, 'I swear I'll do it!'

A chopper overhead. Frank lets go a couple of imaginary rounds; more shrugs from the cops.

A detective steps forward, holds up a white handkerchief.

'Eh,' he says, 'Frank? It's Frank, right? I'm Detective Devine. Wanna talk about this?'

Frank steps back, tightens the stranglehold.

'Come on Frank. Why don't you just let her go. She's got kids. How they gonna feel if Mommy doesn't make it home?'

Frank steps back some more.

'Whaddaya say?'

'I say one more step, copper. One more and she get it.'

The first bullet hits Frank's foot. He goes down, reaches into his jacket for his invisibility cloak; then dark; then there they are—the dots—large and luscious and all around. They bounce and rise along the street, and Frank joins in behind.

My Alibi

I am on my way to the cabin; my mind freeing, undoing as the world zips by. Beside me, my alibi. Everyone got one. I cuffed mine to the passenger door and, when they stopped us back at the roadblock, I kept my eyes ahead and the engine running. They asked about the cuffs. 'What's with the cuffs, fellas?' As it happens, there's no law against driving around with a cuffed passenger. 'The cuffs? They're just cuffs,' said my alibi, knowing better than to risk my ire. 'You know, consenting adults.' They weren't overly happy, convinced, but there you go. Free country. 'Right, so,' said one of them, then waved us on. We drove. He was teared up, my alibi, and said something about his mother and an ailment I'd never heard of. 'Lighten up, ' I told him, and the snivelling stopped.

I'd decided to head to the cabin till everything had gone down and something else had captured the news-people's attention. I figured on three days but was keeping an open mind. They get a lead, anything can happen.

I uncuffed him outside Westport, after that song came over the radio about there being nowhere to run to, baby. Big message from Universe. He didn't sing along but I noticed how he shuffled his shoulders. I don't miss stuff like that.

We left the car in Leenane, outside the pub that's the only structure for miles and quadruples as post office, petrol station and convenience store. The owner, Tony, looked up from The Racing Times as we passed the window, and waved us in. 'The man,' he said, a generic term in these parts for Sorry, I don't remember your name. This is not something my alibi would know. 'Stopping for a pint?' said Tony, pint glass in place under the tap. Things were pretty slow. 'Not today, Tony, need to hit the cabin before dark.' 'Fine,' he said, in a way that suggested anything but. 'We'll take some provisions, though. Eggs, bread, bacon.' 'Fine,' he said again.

We took the steep side of Ben Creggan, into the fog. Couldn't see shit, not even the nose on my face. 'Stay close,' I told my alibi, and stay close he did, like we were doing the vertical spoon. The fog thickened with our tandems steps. 'And left,' I'd say, and we'd move forward, pause, 'And right.' Stuff memories are made of. The descent into the forest around Delphi was slow. 'How much fucking further?' said my alibi, after visibility had grown to a couple of feet. 'Just far enough so as you can't find your way back,' I told him. 'We could have saved ourselves a lot of trouble,' he answered.

We arrived at the cabin. It had been a while; the fuchsia had taken over half the deck. Inside, I cranked up the generator and it turned over first time. 'Make yourself at home,' I said. 'We'll be sticking around for a couple of days.' My alibi kind of scoffed but I let it go. He would have been tired from the hike. I laid out the food on the table and checked the cupboard. It was full of tins and, jackpot, and unopened bottle of the old man's Jameson's. My alibi eyed the bottle. 'Go on,' I said, smiled, 'You deserve it.' He cracked the seal and chugged. 'Whoa!' I said. Had to laugh. When he wouldn't stop, I cracked him over the head with the Lee & Perrins; down he went. I got us a couple of glasses, poured. Certain occasions call for certain etiquette. 'To us,' I said. He got up, rubbed his head and took the glass. I didn't foresee any further problems. 'Go ahead, take a look around.' 'You don't mind?' 'No. I'll get the fire going.' He stepped out onto the deck, looked into the trees and took off. I watched from the door, sipped my whiskey. He was soon out of view, what with the bush. I got the fire going then got myself a refill and went outside, pulled up a chair. He came back into view ten or so minutes later, stopped dead, took off left. Back again after twenty, then ten, five. He panted up to the cabin, hands on knees, scratched face. 'Good workout?' I asked. He walked past me without a word, fell back onto the bed. When I got up again he was snoring. I threw a rug over him, put a log on the fire.

I woke him when the food was ready, bacon and beans, 'Grub up,' I said. I joined him on the bed and we ate.

After supper we smoked the last of my Drum and watched logs burn. I could see the flames dancing in his eyes; shadows licked his face. We were both tired, I guess, after the day we'd had. We finished off the whiskey and I made a mental note to remind the old man to pick up some more. I wondered how he was doing, if everything had gone down okay. I'd fire up the short wave in the morning. Think about my next move. If the weather held up we could go on a hike. Or even head to the pub for the afternoon.

The chopper woke us, approaching. My alibi lifted his head from my lap, returned it there and sighed. I ran my fingers through his hair, thick and strong. 'And now?' he said. He said something else but I couldn't hear over the noise. The cabin was full of wind and light and the voice saying how we should come out with our hands on our heads.

Time itfuckingself

calmed to null & sans.

Every syllable was
fifteen rounds

with Hagler.

Homecoming

When I left the slammer I had enough money for the bus the hell out of there and a can of Dr Pepper. The Dr Pepper was something I'd been looking forward to; the bus ticket would get me as far as mother and my parole officer. If I'd been a more diligent prisoner I could have earned some cash working at the prison call center—and improved my self-esteem by default, they said in the brochure. Delta and United had contracts at the time but it was too weird. 'One-way to Rio, sir? What dates, please?' That's not a job for an inmate. Others took it seriously, though. The going rate was $2 a day, which I suppose if multiplied by fifteen years minus time off for good behaviour—because you're on the phone all day and not horsing around in the yard—amounts to a weekend on The Strip (or more likely Downtown). Also, I was only incarcerated for three years this time, so really, what was the point? There weren't really other ways to generate income without exchanging bodily fluids, and I was saving myself for her. The issue of disposable $ would have to be addressed at a later date. It was like it was predestined—going home and what happened then—it had to happen.

She was all I could think of, all the way home: the girl with the skinny legs and the funny face. It was the first thing I asked mother—was she still in town? Had she married? I was afraid she had forgotten me. Mother sighed, turned out the gas under the pot and sat down. She lit up and blew smoke at the ceiling. Listen up good, she said. Yes, she was still in town. Yes, she'd married. A librarian from Hicksville, years before. And theirs was a happy marriage, people said. They had a daughter—Katy—and a Yorkshire Terrier called Tomahawk. Mother said he was the meanest mutt in town. Now let that be the end of it, she said. You don't want to go there.

But it wasn't to be the end of it, by far, not yet. There was room for more before the final credits rolled: room for comedy perhaps, for action and adventure and—dare I say—room enough for romance. I had not given up hope.

Mother dished the soup and we ate in silence, we'd covered the important ground. I passed on a second serving and she smoked another; I flicked through the paper. She crushed the butt and looked up, Key's in the glove, she said, and stood to clear the bowls. So, I said, catch you later. I need to check in with my parole officer. You do that, she answered, and stay the hell away from her.

Procedure is following, said Smith. You sign here every day for the next three months. You've been released into your mother's custody and that's where I expect to find you after 9p.m., every evening, and no goddamn exception, clear? As for Sophie Whitehall: she knows you're out. Go within four hundred yards of her and, well, that's it: your third strike, you know what that means. Okay. I stood to leave, though he didn't get up, just swirled around in his fancy chair, the end of his glasses stuck in his gob like a pipe. I asked him if there was anything else. Don't fuck up, he said, and scratched his chin like he had something on his mind. It was a Wednesday, hanging in the middle of the week like No Man's Land

I swung by her place on the way home, crawled by at five mph. There was a swing on the front lawn, and an overturned pram. The lawn looked like it could use some work. But otherwise, seemed I'd have to come back.

Back home, mother was passed out in front of the TV. She had the local news channel on mute, and David Bowie's 'Kooks' ripping from the cassette player. I took a blanket from the bedroom and threw it over her. The bottle of gin on the table was less than half empty\full; whichever way you want to look at it, some things just don't change. I sat around for a while, listening to Bowie and watching the weather report. Then I rang her place—five or six times over the space of an hour—but nobody picked up. On the way out I put my head around the door of my old room, it looked like the dust monster had taken over.

I drove over and parked outside. There were lights on, and a couple of shadows moved back and forth in the living room window, frantically, like they were late setting the table and guests were on the way. I guessed Tomahawk was responsible for the yapping, then the yelp, like someone had applied a foot to his side. I gave my next move some thought, or was doing so when light streamed out the front door, and announced her husband—I presume—who came striding across the grass with a hammer in his hand and intent on his face. Before I could unbuckle he'd opened the door and dragged me out of the car. She'd certainly found herself a specimen. Ex-marine I reckoned, who wouldn't have looked amiss back in the yard; fit, strong, not like the last dull sluggard. And not like any librarian I ever knew. He hit me three, four, five times—pounded—and blood ran into my eyes. Then he stopped, just as I was on the verge of losing the ghost. Don't do the crime if you can't do the time; one of the gems of wisdom I learned inside. He looked back to the door, and that's when I caught him between the legs. Self-defence—those were the words ticking in my head as I pried away the hammer and made shit of him. He wasn't so brave now, being dead and all. I recognised the scream and turned to the door. There she was. I lifted a hand in greeting. She'd changed of course; the woman not the girl. And looking the better for it—for the years. Same this and that and everydamnthing. It felt like all my yesterdays. The noise coming out of her stopped but she kept right on screaming big silent screams. It's me, I said and walked towards her, trying to wipe the blood from my eyes. She didn't so much as look at me though, and stumbled around me to where he lay bleeding up the street. It was then I saw the shadow beside the door. Who do we have here? I said, and she peeped her head out. The cutest little girl I ever seen. Well now, I said, and lowered myself to her latitude. You must be Katy. The cutest little thing. What did you do to Daddy? she said, and stepped back. Thing was, I could hear sirens approaching and felt a whole lot of trouble coming my way, more than you could shake a stick at. So instead of getting all wound up in detail, I just lifted her onto my arm and made for the car. This was not part of my original plan, which escapes me now. But hell, I'd make a damn good ersatz father. As we drove away she looked out the rear window and waved to her mommy, who looked a mess—smeared crimson and kneeling in the street, her hands outstretched like she was invoking the Almighty. I watched her in the rear view, then turned south and hit the gas.

Itchy Teeth

I'll usually get some nuts in, a little dried fruit, when the kids come home. And whatever salad's in season. I mix the whole lot up in a bucket out back, with Mayo, sugar, and, my secret—a soupspoon of cayenne pepper. We like our meat fresh, and if we can't find none we do without, no matter how much my teeth are itching for it. The boys always bring sour dough, they live above the best bakery in the city. You should see the line, like they're giving that shit away.

Generally we'll just have one martini 'cause the kids've gotta drive, but sometimes... like when everyone's here, and it's a holiday? We'll put away a bottle or maybe more of Sambuca. Or something exotic. It gives us a faraway type of feeling and we can pretend we don't live in this shithole. Ouzo's good, too. There's this other stuff Janet brought back from the conference in Hungary, Slivovitz? Or anyway, whatever's around the house.

Then we'll get naked and do our body camouflage, just so the neighbours won't see us running around and get excited. It's a gated community, you can't be too careful, people talk. By the time midnight comes around we're pretty much loaded and good to go. I got the spears on ebay, the slingshots at the junk shop. If I can pull the kids off of each other long enough, we'll head out and try to take out a goat or a deer. We haven't got one yet but we're not letting that deter us, they're kind of scarce in the neighbourhood. One'll show, I know it. When we least expect. One time Stu swore he seen an ostrich. Like I said, you never know, so you gotta keep on top of your game at all times. Fruit and nuts is all well and good, but sometimes a girl needs some fresh kill.

Audit/ion

Our hopes were high for the blond. We told her—like we told them all—that the movie was the thing she'd be remembered for; headline news. Our hopes were high, and the audition began; wrong moves, wrong shapes, wrong shadows. We coaxed and encouraged, then railed, and helped her disrobe. Things improved—but not enough to get her the role. We moved on to the next girl and the next after her and the next after her.

*

We'd lost track of numbers and weren't interested in names. The Redhead, someone called her, another wannabe at the crossroads. We took her down to the shore and told her to think of Summer, told her to show us her moves. The whole damn world was grey. Her idea of trying was to not to, understatement; she probably thought we were art house. We told her we'd be in touch, that we wished her well, and that she should enjoy her life. Especially that, enjoy her life. She might never know how close she came to losing it.

*

She knew her shadows and really cast a spell. The roadies loved her but, well, the roadies loved them all. She asked for methadone but settled for grass. We debated her chances, the logistics of getting her out west, then told her Hell, yes, she was the one. Then we took her phone and drugged her. We were confident she could move half a million units.

*

After, we cut her down and posed with the rope, flipped coins to decide who'd get rid of the body. Her tattoo, the piercing, the chipped incisor—all things that could identify her, all things that would have to be disappeared.

After They Got The Word

The walls were three feet thick, the ceiling twelve feet high. The door, though, wasn't soundproof and I could hear them, not trying to hide the fact that they were there, waiting for the word. They paced, whistled and hummed, they even greeted other guests, Alright darling? They'd knocked a couple of times, pretending to be room service, Your champagne, sir, they said, and laughed and fell around till they coughed and I heard them slapping each other's backs. The door was locked. I'd locked it and jammed a chair under the knob, like how they do on TV. I felt better for having made some kind of effort but knew it wouldn't stop them—not these guys—not once the word came. Across the room to the window. I played peek-a-boo behind the curtain, watching the street and the others. A neon arrow flashed directly at the window, almost directly at my head. Not the optimal hiding place. Every quarter hour or so one of them got out of the car, stretched, sometimes even waved to me, to the window. One of them made a pistol with his finger and thumb, pointed up and let go an imaginary bullet. I breathed a sigh, not of relief or respite, more of contentment; soon this would be over. I'd been holed up for three days.

The phone rang, and again and again. Like it had all day. Less rings now than before, eight not twelve. I let it ring out; I wasn't taking calls. I watched him hang up in the car below, then redial. I picked up. Silence. I hung up, it rang again. *Yes.* First the silence, then breathing in my ear, then they were coming through the door. I made it as far as the fire escape, the phone still in my hand. Tell them to back off, I screamed into the phone. They backed off, snarling, spitting, kicking furniture. Tell them to leave. They turned, they left, adjusting ear-pieces and speaking into sleeves. Where is it? he said. Someplace, I said. Tell me where. He entered and lowered the phone, pulled up a chair and lit a Pall Mall. Sit. I walked to the window. So don't sit. It takes me six minutes to smoke one of these and that's as long as you have. Okay, boss? said one of them from the door. Just dandy, he said. This won't take long, wait outside.

His ears resembled orange peel, a thing I hadn't noticed until now. He sucked on the cigarette, examined the nails at the end of his bratwurst fingers and began the tirade. How could you …why… after all… Nothing original, and looking at him sitting there, that's all I really wished for: something original, or at least something new, anything. Bratwurst number one jabbed holes in the air between us like a metronome, Cocksucker, prick, fucking-this-and-fucking-that. So I'd let the man down; point taken. So I'd cheated him; boofuckinghoo.

It will look like suicide, he said. Three floors, happens. He held the cigarette up and looked around for an ashtray. You quit? he said. Fuck me, wonder of wonders, cocksucker quit. He flicked the ash into his hand and shook his head. Wouldn't want to make a mess. I reached for the drawer. Easy, he said, slipping his hand under his jacket. Easy. You want it or not? I said. It's here? You want it? No fucking games, I'm warning you. I opened the drawer, slow. Don't fuck with me, he said. Don't make it worse. The last thing he said. One in the neck, one in the gut. I reached under his jacket and took his 38. I turned to the door and braced myself.

Finding Lunula

She chewed at her fingers and her fingers bled. From across the classroom I watched her smear blood across the tip of her tongue then sit back, calm for a while. The others showed no interest, their faces in their books and out windows. She was new, arrived from a place she never mentioned. Mentioning wasn't her thing; neither talking nor mixing; she was though, it seemed, a cutter. She'd catch my stare and stop, her teeth still deep in cuticle; she'd hold my stare and tear further, pull back more skin till one of us looked away.

When I approached her in the corridor, outside class or in the yard, she'd swerve and blank me, maybe raise a raw finger and hiss through crimson teeth, one time she held a finger to her mouth and gagged.

One Friday when I couldn't stop myself anymore I followed her to the gate of her house and stood in her way and pulled up my sleeves. Blade? She asked. Knife, I said and opened the hand where it sat. Blade, she said, What you need is a blade to get it flowing.

It became like me and her were a population of two.

We went to hers after school and drank pints of aspirin, Thins the blood, she said, Pints of Aspiring. Then we'd scratch and bite. She'd point here, me there and that was it. She'd say stirring me was easier than stirring coffee and bite me till I bled. So it went till one of us said Stop, till someone said 'Nuf. Then we'd lie on the bed and smoke fags as if we'd been screwing.

It was weeks before she told me about lunula. We were smoking and she was examining my fingers as often she did. You're going to be okay, she said. You're going to lead an enchanted life. The fuck you on about? I said. Your whole life is written on your nails, she said—Look here, your lunulae. My, huh? Lunula, she said. The half-moon at the bottom of the nails, it dictates how well you'll deal with crap and yours is fuller than any I've ever seen. Bollocks, I said, The fuck did you read that? You'll see, she said. And then she held her scarred fingers to my face. None; the skin was chewed back further than was good for her but no half-moons. Weird, I said. Yeah, said she, Fucking right, like a sky without a moon.

I didn't step up to blades right away. That first day she came back from the bathroom and held it up. Dad's, she said, Unused, and placed it beside the fishbowl where it lay for a month. What are their names? I asked. Fish don't have names, she said and squeezed a drop of blood into the water.

Then, that day. She picked it up, said, May I? Course, I said and lay back on the bed and she started tracing the veins on my arms with her nail, then with the blade, parallel to the veins like a blood bath on a dual carriageway. Usually I went home by dark but that night things got late. Time escaped out the window and into the sky and the last thing on my mind as I lay there having my arms opened was my mother but there she was when the door opened, stood on the landing with fuck knows—her old man, I think, brothers, and the lot of them shrieking their gills out and tearing at their hair. That's what started us too, and what with the drama, the blade twisted deeper.

I came to, hooked up to a drip and strapped down. Pale bedside parents not looking like they'd had much sleep. The fuck? I said and my mother up and left in tears, the old man behind her. The fuck? I said again and good thing the brother was there. Did we have a suicide pact? he wanted to know. The fuck? She lost it when she thought she'd done me in, he said, and, well, ended it, end of story. Almost end of story—there was one last stop, the funeral parlour the next evening. She looked different, I don't know, larger, just different. Some knob had wrapped a rosary beads around her hands, her fingers. The fingers looked well, probably touched up with something. I held her face and blew a hair from her eyes. Her cuticles had retracted in death and there they were—her lunulae. They looked like surfboards and flying saucers and hand grenades and I thought and wondered, and wished she could have been there.

Propulsion

He saw the first dim stick figures, watched them gather on the pier off starboard, no doubt full of brew at this hour. He paused to draw breath, then took in the oars and pulled out the pouch, rolled a cig as the sea gently turned him and pointed him away, offshore. The sea knew best if you listened. He struck a match but it was damp, as was the next one, as were they all. He spat and cursed then put back the pouch. Oar in oarlock, swish, exhale. The dark glass of sea; waves from the pier, barely visible. *Ahoy,* someone called. If only they knew. *Ahoy.* Then fast loud words, pointing, calls and quiet; retreat. All but one, who sucked on a pipe and sighed at the arriving narrative.

Oar in oarlock, swish, exhale; the sound of propulsion now part of him, coaxing the currach home. The phoenix on his chest was a turkey-necked burlesque dancer, her skirt aflame, her eyes on the coastline. Not long now. He leaned into another stroke.

We have our myths, they'd said, our story. Ours. They flashed anchors and ships, Neptune with coiled deep-sea denizens. Take the wind that brought her here, and be gone. Back to your mother's cave. Be gone or—

He'd pretended not to hear, then to mishear, then the world asunder and he was lucky to flee. Oar in oarlock, swish, exhale; down the years.

The final stroke.

You shouldn't have come, the old man said. Good to see you too. The old man stooped to help pull the currach ashore. He shushed him away. The phoenix stirred and the dancer stretched. Ash now all around, in his mouth and in his very words. And heat, rising, bigger than the years.

Telescopia

In this one, a grainy black and white, you look a lot like Anne Frank, and I remember you saying how much you enjoyed her diary, insofar-all-considered. Consider: That time I came home and found you in a closet, how you scrunched your face and shushed me, then tiptoed west, from A to B—B being the farthest point away, within the confines of these walls. Later, tearing downstairs, shrieking *"Do you see that I am your friend? Can you see that you will always be my friend?"* Dances With Wolves—I mean, who didn't see it? Your brother ('Shame I don't get to give you a kicking') dropped by for your stuff. It took him six hours to tick everything off the list and drink my beer. I'll never believe you forgot the album—you left it—and even now, sometimes, I'll squeeze into the closet and browse. The one where you look like a spinning top; the one with the cracked grey eyes; the one in the snow—how you said snow was boring and disgusting. My favourites, though, are of your shadow, but then like now I think of him, holding the camera, then later holding you.

At My Sister's Wedding

At my sister's wedding: the bride wore lemon, the groom wore Armani, and both of them looked damn fine. The High Priest showed up with the key at a minute to ten, and if looks could kill nine lives would be no good to him. Waiting in the burning sun didn't bother us so much, but his suit—the colour of cooked lamb's liver, did.

At my sister's wedding: we, thirty of us, crammed into the Registry Office to hear them say they would. There were lousy acoustics and my brother shouted 'speak up' from the back. And they did. It's always him at the back, the deaf guy, no matter what the occasion. My sister wore red high heels and as we left my other sister produced a tape recorder from thin air and blasted us with Tom Wait's 'I love the way she looked in those red shoes.' We did, too.

At my sister's wedding: we walked to the hotel restaurant and I complained personally to the manager about there being no red carpet. As he retreated I heard him mutter 'fucking royalty' under his breath, and I told him he'd better watch his step sunshine, or else. He did the honourable though, and took the rest of the day off, leaving us in the capable hands of Charlie, the maitre d'.

At my sister's wedding: Charlie served bubbly, and at the same time handed my sister her presents, one by one. The man was mercurial, and I made a mental note to keep him in mind if ever I should take the plunge myself, though as he was fairly getting on in years, he probably wouldn't make it.

At my sister's wedding: one of the nine year olds threw a screaming tantrum till she was allowed 'grown up' champagne. My sister turned on the waterworks when she saw the Waterford Crystal photo frame I got them. Works every time.

At my sister's wedding-lunch: most people went with the shrimp cocktail followed by steak in pepper sauce. Mum had the melon & parma ham; dad smoked while we ate, and nobody batted an eyelid. I had the ostrich. My sister had the duck.

At my sister's wedding: the hotel eventually gave me a new room after I informed them that the one they'd given me stank to high heaven of fire damage. My girlfriend shook her head a lot that day, and told me to lighten up.

At my sister's wedding: my new brother-in-law's brother said a few words and that was the end of the speeches. My father only does eulogies, and I'd already stirred enough shit.

At my sister's wedding: we planned to retire for naps after lunch, and meet again at 7 in the lobby, casual attire. But Happy Hour was beginning next door, so nobody bothered. We share a collective fondness for the juice.

At my sister's wedding: after Happy Hour our parents jived. You should have heard those bongos go-go. It was the first time we had ever seen them touch, and there are photos to prove it. We also tried to get a photo of just the siblings together, but my mother got her mug in every shot. A while later, thinking the power failure or blackout was restricted to my personal grid, I didn't utter a goddamn word, but was secretly relieved when the bar-staff distributed candles. I was in no mood for another visit to the medicine man.

At my sister's wedding: after the bar closed we started on our party pieces. My father sang Lilly Marlene, I sang the first verse of Puff The Magic Dragon—in German, and the band played the National Anthem. Everybody stood and swayed to attention except my other brother-in-law who's a Jehovah's Witness, and doesn't recognise nation states in the large scheme of things. We thought the locals might lynch him. Looking back, I guess he was the real patriot.

It must have been 2 a.m. before the braves got back with the kill, to my sister's wedding. But we had that baby hung and skinned in no time. What a beauty. We toasted the newlyweds with a warm cup of the lioness blood; the younger ones smoked a pipe. And then we slept.

At my sister's wedding: nobody noticed the bump in the lemon dress that we would later christen Shauna-Kate. What a gift. What a day.

The Story in The Shoe-box

'See this, can you believe this shit? Five bucks was all the guy wanted, five bucks!'

I'd read about this in the travel guide—don't be alarmed when random strangers, not just homeless people, address you like they know you. He put the shoe-box down on the table and pulled up a seat.

'Lemme tell you pal, it's my lucky day. There must be a thousand pictures in here. A thousand!'

He opened the shoebox and rummaged through photographs. Taking a handful, he emptied them into the lid. Then, one at a time, he started to hold them up for inspection.

An hour before, Andrea and I had checked into a hotel on Cyril Maginin. She opted for a bath and shut-eye after the long flight, but my feet were itching for San Francisco.

'Don't talk to any strange men,' she said, 'and bring me back a blueberry muffin.' Blueberry muffins are hard to come by in Europe.

I got all of two blocks before I stopped for coffee. And now this, my first authentic American, with a shoe-box full of a stranger's photographs.

'Will you look at the hair on these broads? That's exactly how my aunty Pattie used to wear hers, you know, up like that. Jeez, this takes me back. Hey, look, writing, what's that say?' He squinted and held the photo close.

'Can't see a goddamn thing, I know—wait till you see this,' he said, and pulled a pair of glasses from the shoe box. They had a purple, butterfly frame and one lens was missing. 'The guy threw them in for free,' he said. 'I didn't buy them or nothing.'

'I believe you,' I said, noting the exits.

'There you go,' he said, balancing the glasses on the end of his nose, and read,

'Catherine, Charlie, Sol. Will you look at these guys, flyers for sure.' Charlie and Sol were in uniform. 'Don't you love black and white? My money says Cathy and Sol are an item, as are Charlie and the lady who took this shot. In fact, maybe she took all these shots. Whaddaya say?'

'Could be,' said I, 'could be.'

'What about these uniforms? Korea maybe? Or World War 2?

'World War 2,' I said.

'Yeah, I think you're right pal, good call.'

'Hey! Here she is, – me and Charlie, Atlantic City '58, that's my girl. Look at her, isn't she the looker?'

She was.

'The studious type, and not many broads took an interest in photography back then, goes to show you. Hey—the glasses! She's wearing my goddamn glasses!' He threw his head back and laughed, 'What the fuck!'

'I wonder what her name was?' I said.

'Well, keep on looking, we'll find it, you wait and see.'

We trawled through pictures but didn't find a name. There were lots of the two of them together, from 'Charlie and me—young love,' to 'Me and Charlie at the condo'. On the back of the wedding photograph, 'Mr and Mrs King,' but no first name, down all the years, to 'Charlie's retirement party.'

'No first name. And look at those eyes, those eyes spell p-a-i-n.'

It was true, she did look sad. 'How about a coffee?' I said.

'No, I gave up, bad for you. You go ahead though.'

'I didn't catch your name,' I said.

'Because I didn't I tell you. Theo Doyle, nice to meet you. Where you from, kid?'

'Ireland.'

'Holy shit,' said Theo Doyle, 'me too, man, the old country.'

Again, the travel guide had warned me—nobody is just American, they're Irish American, African American, ad infinitum-American.

'You been to Ireland?' I asked.

'Hell, no,' said Theo, 'but maybe one day. Good y'all finally got your shit together over there—the war's over, right?'

I nodded.
'You tried the bacon and cabbage at O'Reilly's? Lemme tell ya kid, it's out of this fucking world. Hey, look here, Geraldine. Isn't she the cutest baby you ever seen?'
She was adorable.
'See that? Cloth diapers, it wasn't easy back then.'
'What do you do with them all, Theo?' I asked.
'The pictures?' said Theo, looking at me like he felt sorry for me, 'well, I look at them.' He turned half away and crossed his legs, 'What's wrong, you think that's weird, or something?'
'No. I was just curious if you were an artist or something. I thought maybe you made collages or something,' I said, regretting I hadn't held my tongue.
'Collages?' said Theo, looking more disturbed by the second.
'Ehh, yeah, when you cut stuff up and-'
'I know what a collage is,' said Theo. 'Cut them? Cut up these beautiful photographs? What kind of weirdo would do such a thing?' All of a sudden, now that his eyes had narrowed and he was wringing his hands, Theo Doyle looked quite menacing.
'Hey, listen, I'm sorry man, really, I wasn't trying to … shit, I don't know. It's just, I've never met anyone who, well, buys shoe-boxes full of strangers' photographs.' Shut up, I was saying to myself. This guy is going to lose it any second.
Theo made a fist and held it up for inspection. He turned it around and looked at it from all sides.
'I should be going,' I said.
Theo slapped his thigh and laughed. 'Ha! Irish! Had you going there, huh? You should see the look on your face, hahaha. Boy, like I was gonna pull a knife or something. Priceless.'
'Yeah,' I said, 'but really, it's time I was-'
'Jesus!' shouted Theo Doyle and slapped his forehead.
'What? What is it?'
'Help me here, kid.' He dropped a handful of pictures in front of me.
'What are we looking for?'

'Geraldine, that's what, the baby. Here's one, baby's first step, keep on looking.'

'Theo, there are tons of baby snaps.'

We laid them all to one side, fifty, maybe more.

'See what I mean?' said Theo.

'Only baby pictures,' I said.

'You're a bright kid,' said Theo. 'No first day at school, no birthdays, no First Communion. Baby Geraldine never made it.'

'It looks that way.'

Polio, that's what I reckon, maybe TB.'

'Poor thing,' I said.

'Yeah,' said Theo Doyle, 'tough break for Mrs King. So much for three-score-years-and-ten.'

'Yeah,' I said, ' we don't all get it.'

'I gotta go,' said Theo, and gathered up the shoe-box and its contents. 'Here, keep this one, a souvenir.' He handed me a picture of a young Charlie at the wheel of a Buick. 'Enjoy the city,' he said, 'and say hello to the Old Country, say hello from Theo Doyle.'

Bony Bear

'Bony bear.'

'No! Really?'

'Yup. Bony bear.'

She leapt from the bed. So much for the dodgy knee.

'Finally! Let me see. Anyway you have to say it outside, come on…'

'Huh?'

'*Bony bear*, you have to say it outside in the snow like Fleischman and Maggie and all the others did, you know that. Come on ..... Yes, at last! BONY BEAR!'
We stood on the balcony, it wasn't quite light yet. Andrea in pyjamas, eyes full of sleep. I watched as she did her little victory dance, NFL style. Like every year.
'Bony bear, Bony bear, Bonne eee-bear, Bonne hiver!'
Winter's first snow; cause for celebration, of sorts. Just like every year, it's our tradition.
'Those accents were the worst ever. Why were they anyway trying to speak French? I mean, Northern Exposure was set in Alaska, no?' She knew my answer:
'You always ask that. I have no idea.' She has a point, though.
'Thank you for keeping this tradition, especially ..... I understand that you don't want to celebrate this year, that it's too early. But, well, it's my favourite time, Advent and ... Chri ... you know.'
'I'd noticed. And it's okay to say the word, it's not going to change anything. Christmas isn't going away.'
'But you still don't mind us putting up decorations, do you? Just maybe some fairy lights out here on the balcony? It's okay that you

don't sign the Christmas cards. I can understand that. Can you check for mail? Why haven't I got any cards yet? BONY BEAR! I saw a light, do you think I woke the neighbours? Shall we go to the Eck Haus this evening and have goose and dumplings, like we do every year? I know, but we're not even giving each other presents this year, it could be our treat. It's what she'd want. She'd want us to be happy. I know that's what she'd want.'

My head fell and the tears fell.

'Hey. You miss her, don't you? I know, I miss her too. We all do. Nobody ever thought we'd be having Christmas without her. It's not easy. It must be horrible for your father, there alone.'

Sobbing now, on her shoulder, tears and snot and snow.

She stroked my hair and whispered low, '*But still. Bony bear.*'

The Farmers of An Líonán

Wednesday is Poker Night in the hamlet of An Líonán. Locals gather in the pub—the schoolteacher, the priest, the shop-owner/mayor, a retired professor and a half dozen housewives and widows—and wait for the farmers to arrive, down from the hills of Connemara. The farmers speed along the Old Bog Road to avoid the musical chairs that takes place before the first hand is dealt. Last man arriving gets to sit with the priest, two widows, and the professor. Father Pat is the problem. Haven't seen you of a Sunday this good while, Pat, Seán, Michael, Diarmuid, Caoimhín, Dáithí, etcetera. The land, Father—work, is the standard reply; but no one likes lying to a priest.

The couple dozen card players drink inky pints, exchange news, and continue old conversations.

~

In The Year of Crazy Weather it snowed September thru Christmas thru Easter. As the farmer had no money for feed, he slaughtered his milk cows and sold them to a factory that produced gelatine. Each cow had had a name. He could tell one from the other by the topography of veins and warts on their teats. When the weather changed again, that summer, the farmer started over. He invested in new cows, the beginnings of what became the largest herd west of The Shannon. He was never the same though, people liked to say, his eyes never shone like they had before.

~

The farmer would say A day I don't get dirt under my nails is a lost day. He couldn't remember where he'd got that from—he had not always wanted to be a farmer. As a boy, having seen David Niven in Casino Royale, he had wanted to be a croupier in Monte Carlo, or a jewel thief. He couldn't remember deciding to become a farmer, and in fact he hadn't—one day he was the last sibling, the others dead or gone, and his destiny was sealed.

~

The farmer said, claimed, that his border collie had overheard him say he was the smartest dog ever. And that the next morning the dog left the farm for America, stowawayed, changed his name to Colin and went to Harvard where he studied Law. By the time Colin had become a full partner in a Chicago law firm, mortal embarrassment was all he felt when he remembered the farm. The sheep; all that running. He was repulsed by lamb and would vomit at the mention of the word mutton. Colin met a nice girl, Jean, a secretary at the firm, whose great grandmother had been one of the Egans of Ballymote, direct descendants of the druids. Jean gave birth to three healthy puppy-humans. Colin was happy; they were happy; they bought a big place out in the country. Colin enjoyed a successful career and rose to the position of judge. For a while there was talk of The Republican Ticket. He'd been the smartest dog ever, the farmer said, just not the best sheepdog.

~

The farmer was observing the stars the night he was abducted by aliens. He was gone for forty two seconds but it felt like a hundred years. His abductors were mauve, translucent, and had the consistency of cheddar. They were kind and polite, inquisitive about life on the farm. When, afterwards, the farmer told people about his time in the outer reaches, they ridiculed him. But it was only when his wife went back to her mother that he stopped sharing. Evenings, he'd sit by the fire—pipe in hand, cat in lap—and reminisce. He likened his abduction to going on vacation, a thing he had never done, but something he planned to consider in the future.

~

He sank the spade and cut the turf, withdrew the spade and sank it again, fashioned bricks of fuel that he tossed to the side. Miles and miles of bog; his inheritance. Honest work, the farmer told himself, or had told himself, not anymore. There'd been a settlement here, of Bronze Age Celts perhaps, he wasn't sure, but why else would the professor have offered him so much for the land? The farmer dreamed of ancient treasure—a broach or a hairclip, a wristband.

He worked faster now—sank the spade, cut the turf; a fury inside that mirrored the sky.

When the farmer joked that his chickens laid golden eggs, people understood the metaphor. The day a chicken laid an actual golden egg, the farmer keeled over and died. It was the same day his wife brought over the divorce papers. When she found the farmer and the egg, she made the necessary calls about the former, then searched the house for her passport.

There used to be money in tubers but people didn't eat like that anymore. There were some lean years for the farmer. Then came the visit from the fast food people. The Humble Spud, they called it—baked or scalloped, fries. Never heard of you, the farmer said, then entered his bank account details and signed. They sent a crew of six to re-till and plant, all the latest gear—it was like an effin John Deere convention. The farmer had never had it so good. Things stayed good for a long time after.

The farmer's staples were minced beef with onions and potatoes and, since people didn't eat them anymore: pig's trotters, ox-tail and cow's tongue. Plus no shortage of dairy, plus a feast of Guinness on Poker Night. The doctor shook his head, Six months if you're lucky—but we'll make you comfortable, I promise you won't feel a thing. I won't feel a thing? said the farmer. Nothing. How long if I go home? Eight weeks, tops, said the doctor. Good luck so, said the farmer, and pulled back the sheet.

~

The farmers worried about what was coming, not in the Hereafter, but in the Here and Now—who would work the land? They could not see themselves in their sons. It was more than the start of a new millennium, something fundamental had changed. They knew, too, what it was; or, rather, they knew what it was called: Digital Revolution. World Wide Web. All of the farmers agreed on this.

~

The sheep found at the foot of Bin Creggan was marked with orange, yellow, blue, red, green and pink paint—each splash another farmer's marking. Mine. One Wednesday in November these six farmers found themselves seated at one poker table. The odds were incredible. There had never been a quieter table in all the history of Poker Night, until the final hand that decided who would win.

~

The farmer famed for his poitín had turned yellow. I'm not well at all, he told anyone who'd listen. People smiled, thought And whose fault is that? After he died from complications following jaundice, everyone spoke well of him.

~

The farmer needed money for his youngest's Confirmation. There'd have to be a dress and a veil and shoes and a handbag and God only knew. There would have to be a trip to Dublin to procure, and a night at Jury's Inn and all that that entailed. Perhaps they'd take in a show at The Gaiety, or a film. Cursed money. The farmer sold Gráinne, his prize milk cow—she was the only one who'd bring enough—to the Hegartys of Tuam, a clan he despised though he never said why. Grainne lived four more years and her milk—and the cheese and butter made from it—went on to win national and international prizes.

~

A time came when people stopped referring to the farmer as single, and started calling him a bachelor. He hadn't told anyone, yet, about his brother's plan to import a Russian woman for him to marry. He was unsure; bachelorhood wasn't a bad gig, but the brother meant well.

~

The kids weren't coming back, they had other lives now: jobs and families across the sea, mortgages to be paid. But one of them could have stayed, the farmer said. And all of them could have stayed closer, not running out the door at eighteen. It wouldn't be long before he was too old or infirm to travel. And in the meantime there was work; the land wouldn't take care of itself.

~

The farmer hadn't drunk since the All-Ireland Hurling Final in 1987. Galway 1-12, Kilkenny 0-9.

The game, the banter—everything was epic. He'd had a skin-full of pints before switching to Jameson's. The next day wasn't good—the farmer woke to find that his wife had left him, and taken his three beautiful daughters: Aoife, Sive and Caitlin. The farmer had forgotten much more than he would ever remember.

~

The priest, Father Pat, had been posted to An Líonán from a parish in Dublin. 1993. He never thought of the city now, and hadn't been back since his sister's funeral in '98. He liked The West and was happier than ever before. His parish had six hundred souls and covered twenty-eight square miles. A day didn't pass without him administering one of the sacraments; although, down all the years, he had never heard one farmer's confession.

~

The farmer woke early to tend his cows. This day was different, however, as in the night he'd lost his love for the land. He walked down the hill and into An Líonán, and when the pub opened he sat up at the bar and that's where he could be found for the next five months, opening hours permitting. In this time his farm went to ruin. When the farmer hadn't been seen or heard from in four days, the pub owner stopped by his cottage to see how he was, and found him swinging from a beam in the barn.

Ink

Surer

now.

I've broken all my pencils

The Body Language of Trees

The Body Language of Trees moves off, mounts zigzag. From the ridge he calls below, 'Suchness kills relations,' but the words etherise and the Maharajah of Connemara does not hear. The Maharajah of Connemara refuses to unshoe. The hills know pain, says The Body Language of Trees, they feel each hobnailed step, now get over yourself and unshoe. I won't, says The Maharajah of Connemara, and nips from a flask.

The Body Language of Trees accepts his invitation and arrives at 2 p.m. sharp. He has a bath full of 90% spudstilled hooch. The Body Language of Trees joins him in the bathroom where they sit on the lip of the tub and drink. A soft day, this, rain irretrievable mist. Later, the two of them empty the house of its furniture, into the garden with it, then strip naked and wrestle.

The Body Language of Trees drinks tea. A good day, this, he says, and toasts sheep in misty hills. The salmon oblige—a raging horde of onetrack mind, pink and gold in mauve Connemara.

A battalion of sheep stealth down on a sleepdoze Body Language of Trees. One licks his hand, another chews his laughter. They gather round like kids for stories. The Body Language of Trees peels back skin and embraces a bloodshot afternoon; chops and liver, a fair pot of stew.

Christmas in November. This won't do, she says, on waking, and extricates what she can. Better you'd smothered me, better I'd ignited on impact. The Body Language of Trees stands—his neck wilts and his shoulders round. From the side he is a question mark.

A dozen baby steps and the ocean sinks and he kicks without wanting. The Body Language of Trees is followed into the waves by Sasha, a pastel pink Golden Retriever. Don't even think about it,

Sasha says, and chomps a foot, paddles him home. The Body Language of Trees coughs his way back, forward, call it what. Ashore, Sasha performs CPR then bounds the beach after a tennis ball.

The Body Language of Trees deposits himself at the roundabout which is the last chance to not continue West into Connemara. Locals stop and say Christ, Body, this is no weather, get in before you catch a dose. He waves them on, prefers The Gulf Stream to fireside pints. Tourists approach in rentals and he flags them down, tells them Connemara is closed, that There is nothing to see here, folks, just Feck Off. The Body Language of Trees considers this his Civic Duty.

Crushed Ice

The rapist-thoughts
were ever present.
Sorry, *therapist*; typo.

We went to
preliminary ice-
breaking sessions
all over town

a.m.

today's disaster movie
in production
on the burner,

simmering brown
in tinfoil

Graphologizing

They'd missed each other, had passed each other by with precision. Minutes were windows to escape through and nothing was wrong until verbalized.

They communicated via Post-its, stuck them on the mirror in the hallway. Cancellations mostly, but reminders, too—the tax return, a signature. The notes grew shorter, elliptical; the handwriting poor. His resembled Morse; hers, Miro. Her final note is blank; and he knows that she is gone.

Her note on the mirror. Its blankness reminds him of her absence. It falls to the floor six, maybe seven weeks later and he knows she isn't coming back. Her letter falls through the door the next day.

He'd assumed she was with friends. Or her mother. The stamp suggests not.

He rereads the letter—trawls through it in a different light, a different room. Slants, loops, dots; he searches, feels the indentations through the page. He thinks about her choice of words. He empties the glass and goes out for air. Back home, he retrieves the letter from the bin. He rereads, trawls through it in a different room, a different light.

He drafts a reply in his head. He drafts at dinner, and later in the bath. The drafts grow shorter. A page, then less. He drafts as he lies in bed. Shorter each time. He sets the clock for seven, drafts. It's clear now, everything he has ever wanted to tell her; one sublime sentence, scratched across his mind.

He sleeps, parts of him sleep. His mind works on the draft. By two a.m., all that remains is four words. By five *p.m.*

dim-time, quiet,
everybody
drunk on books/
miscellaneous

Exit

'Gelato,' she says. ' I want gelato.' First words since morning.

I check my watch, shake my head and busy myself with traffic. We'll never make check-in.

'Gelato,' she says again, the vowels longer. She points to the exit, keeps her arm outstretched. I puff my cheeks but follow her finger and we exit the autostrada. I follow her finger onto national roads and secondary roads and roads which aren't roads at all. We stop for gelato. I order a coke and light a cigarette. She orders Stracciatella.

Gelato in hand, she looks back the way we've come. The mountains are out of view, her village.

'Stracciato,' she says.

'Stracciatella?' I say. 'No, never liked it. Those splinters, shards of chocolate like shrapnel.'

'No,' she says. 'Stracciato. I am torn apart.'

iso-something

He searches for a word, trawls the ocean that's his mind, knowing full well that if his mind were an actual body of water it would be somewhere on a continuum between bed-wetting and designer garden ponds. Those designer garden ponds that come with a plastic Buddha/water feature on a timer. He *trawls*—knowing that the word implies searching for something that likely exists, which may not be the case in his language. (There are words, after all, for concepts that exist in one place and time, and not necessarily in another. Also, words get hijacked and/or adopted—take *amok,* Bahasa Indonesian; take Zeitgeist and Weltschmerz; take me down to the Zuiderzee.) Looking for something that isn't /may not be there might explain why he's adrift on a metaphor, though not why he's adrift on this particular watery example. Unchartered waters. He wishes he could stop it—get off the metaphor-boat, away. Or is it an analogy? Whichever; semantics. Shore Leave. She was his helmsman. Stop it. *The word.* The word which prompted the search should mean—describe, summarise, equate to and be synonymous with: how he feels plotted against the time he feels so. Easy. Feeling vs Time: *iso*-something, like the weather stuff. The prefix is on the money, the *something* will do for now, but there has to be more for the core of the feeling that's missing her. But for now, he charts iso-something on a graph in his head—while eating, while reading, while spinning the dial on the wireless across the tips of his fingers. Iso-something swells with the memories folded around her clothes in the wardrobe, at the bottom of the laundry basket; it surges and breaks with fossilised photographs, and it's there, too, in the cigarettes she left in the galley, in the plants she bought for him to amuse. The something riddles the postcards she sent that show him what and where he might be now. It saturates, then cascades and rumbles through him and his work, his job; the schedules and appointments. Lunch is a sandwich between A and B, where she is the background music, the face looking down from the billboards. Afternoons, reports have to be filed, or signed, stamped and sent.

Answer the phone, send that mail, nod in affirmation and smile at platitudes. Work ebbs then rolls back to reveal city streets, which he follows to the station and the train and the seat by the window. And there she is, in his head but all at sea, waiting. Home, he draws the curtains and falls back on the bed. Memories of their trips and plans, their everyday, but also the tears and venom—the ticket-stubs in the pocket of his gym bag, the shredded shirts after his bogus account of that one weekend. The memories change with each imagining: her hair is long then short; blue jeans, white jeans, no jeans. Her mouth moves but the imaginings are mute. He no longer remembers her voice. He charts the *iso*-something as well as he can. He makes a new graph every evening, spits on the back of it and sticks it to the wall. Each one is an excursion she reaches out from, silent—she invites him to cast off, make one last trip. The salt on the wind and the wind in her hair; that one wavelength they both lived for. The something grows, outside him now. She reaches but he doesn't dare. She stretches. She directs, the imaginings are no longer his. She reaches and at last he grasps, but finds only static. All there is, and he swims. He misses appointments, forgets to send reports. He postpones dates that weren't fixed to begin with or have long since taken place. There is trouble, people complain. Stuff doesn't arrive because stuff wasn't sent. He gets himself a reputation, though he'll never realise, so will never care. He stays home, his course fixed. No one calls. The graphs come loose and fall, like the wrack he has become. He spins the dial on the wireless, listens to Berlin and Luxembourg and Moscow. Then 1520 kHz, Caroline. The signal fluctuates, then smooth across the waves. He turns up the volume till it fills all that is left. Her image is grainy, then strong. She embraces him. Then static, sudden and loud, then not at all, gone.

Acknowledgments

The following stories were previously published, sometimes in slightly different form and with different titles. Many thanks to the readers, editors and publishers of those magazines.

"Graphologizing," (*PANK*), "Saturday in Hackney," (*elimae*), "Nancy Spain," (*Necessary Fiction*), "Cheese Fondue," (*elimae*), "The Orange Grove," (*Juked*), "Crossing," (*elimae*), "Exit," (*elimae*), "The Magic Word," (*Hobart*), "Out of Landshut," *(Everyday Genius)*, "Out of Kitzbühel," *(Indiana Review)*, "At The Neuwiener Hütte" *(Gargoyle)*, "Cyclicismus," (*Spork*), "Lunch," (*elimae*), "Laundry," (*elimae*), "Don't Give Up," (*McSweeney's*), "Shore Leave." (*NANO Fiction*), "While Oliver Paints" (*Necessary Fiction*), Putting Down Roots on Boppard on The Rhein," *(Eyeshot)*, "Mooring," (*Anemone Sidecar*), The Body Language of Trees," *(Birkensnake)*, "Finding Lunula," (*Red Peter*), "Propulsion," (Juked), "Telescopia," (Oblong), "The Water Carrier," *(Gargoyle)*, "When We Needed To Get Out More," (*Blue Print Review*), "The Small Boy and The Big Cat," (*Café Irreal*), "One-way to Rio," (*Dogzplot*), "Afternoon Performance," (*Dogzplot*), "Prelude," (*Fractured West*), "Little Red-haired Girl," (*Juked*), "The Makings of Our Story," (*Johnny America*), "The Love Song of H.R.K. Sommers," (Eyeshot), "The Soundtrack of My Life," (*Spork*), "Algebra and Ali McGraw," *(Pindeldyboz)*, "My Alibi," (*The 2nd Hand*), "Homecoming," (*The 2nd Hand*), "Audit/ion," (Abe's Penny), "Invisible Man," (*Titular*), "A Day Much Like Another," (*Pequin*), "At My Sister's Wedding," (*Pindeldyboz*), "Frank Joins The Dots," (*Juked*), "The Story in The Shoe-box," (*Word Riot*), The Farmers of *An Líonán (Los Angeles Review)*, "iso-something," (*Passages North*), "Algorithm for Meshing Scenarios," *(Vector)*, "The Night of The Fire," (*Permafrost*), "Un Sac Comme Le Mien," *(Gargoyle)*

About the Author

Kevin O Cuinn lives and loves in Frankfurt on The Main. He comes from Dublin, Ireland, and is fiction editor at *Word Riot.*